Lovin' The Wrong Thug 2
By: Kia Meche'

Acknowledgements:

Well I'm back again and first off I wanna give a major thank you to the man above. Without him I would not have the talent to deliver.

My supporters, my readers, you guys are the best and I thank y'all so much for rocking with me so strong. I wouldn't be here if the love y'all show wasn't so strong. Thank you.

To my family that showed love, thank you for believing in me. I love y'all for that.

Sister, we have the best bond ever and I never have to question the love you have for me. You help me anytime I am in need and whether I tell you or not, I appreciate you.

To my honey and Aston, y'all support me thru whatever and give me the drive to keep going. You never lose faith in me and I'm forever grateful.

Hmm, Bestie, my dog, my potna in crime, thank you for all of the support you show. No matter what I do you always show love and support regardless. That's a real friend and you are the best.

Corrie, thanks for being that listening ear when I get stressed cause Lawd knows a chick be stressed writing sometimes.

Tiarra, I recently met you but you 100 and remind me so much of myself. You show mad love and I can't do nothing but salute you on that.

Kellz, Niqua, and Ebony, I know that I work y'all nerves but y'all never get impatient with me and the support is real and genuine. Thank you. #Salute

Charae and my petty twin Jasmine, my other author boos, thank you for believing in me to do what I do. I remember when I first decided to write from reading y'all books and y'all pushed me to go forth. Thank you so much and I appreciate the love.

To my Tiecey, I can't thank you enough for the love you have shown me. I could never thank you enough for taking a chance on me. You show your team love and interact with us and that is what I call a real publisher. You are the best!!

Let me wrap this up because I am really not the emotional type but before I do, to

my #TMP and #RWP FAM, I love all of you and the only way to go is up from here.

We are bread winners and the top looking reallll nice.

FACEBOOK: KIA ASTONSMOM WALTON

IG: MECHE_ASTON

Previously in part one:

I bet y'all didn't know a nigga was the mastermind behind all this bullshit. This bitch Moe thought she was gonna play me and get away with it. You see, I never gave a fuck about the next bitch, when I had a whole wife at home. I played that bitch to orchestrate this whole thing. The bitch set niggas up, so she had to be one dumb bitch to think I would leave my wife for a trifling bitch like that. I had some of my lil niggas shoot King and made everybody think that it was Cody hoping to make them go at each other's head. Drew was just the bait in the whole equation. This nigga King got sidetracked in the midst of my plan because he fell in love with some pussy. I gave Moe the money to give to Moto for putting a hit for Cody's head so he would think it was King. I convinced Moe to get into that nigga Drake's head so that Cody would lose trust in him. I didn't plan on killing Drake, but you not about to be fucking the same bitch I was fucking, under my fucking roof at that. Drake thought I didn't know about him trying to get at my wife a while back, but my bitch told me everything. That shit is disrespectful. I knew all about Dior and Dakota's mother being the bitch that killed my pops, so her time was also limited. Speaking of mothers, Ms. Joyce was on my agenda as well, because she kept my pops from loving me the way a father should have. I was clearing house. Now my problem with my brother was that my pops always praised that nigga when he came around. All I ever heard was how he was getting to the money and how proud he was of him. I was going to take a different approach and talk to the nigga about getting this money together, but fuck that, I would rather just take it all. King thought he had it all figured out, but he ain't have shit. I even had two of his most valuable soldiers on my team against his dumb ass. Cody actually thought I would work up under him when I was a boss nigga my damn self. I brought in more money than he did and that fuck nigga thought I was gonna let that shit slide. He put his trust in me and since I knew his whole operation, I took money that rightfully belonged to me. See, these niggas thought I was some bitch boy that ate crumbs, and I was far from it. I thought that nigga was smarter than the average dummy, but he couldn't even see I was plotting. I got a knock at the door, so I went to see who it was.

"About time y'all niggas got here. What the fuck took so long?"

"The nigga had us waiting and shit, running his fucking mouth."

My cousin Reese and his homeboy Nard were some money hungry niggas you could pay to pretty much do anything. The niggas had it out for King because of some bullshit that popped off at some club a while back, but that wasn't my concern.

We headed back down to the basement.

"Damn boss man, you didn't waste no time popping this nigga, huh?"

I ignored him because I wasn't with the jokes and he was pissing me off.

"What's up nigga?"

The nigga looked at me with murder in his eyes, but that shit put no fear in my heart.

"Who the fuck are you? Fuck that, it don't even matter, but I know y'all fuck niggas better let me go."

"I see Pops raised you right. You got a lot of heart little bro."

"What the fuck you just say to me nigga?

"I said Pops raised you right. Fuck nigga you heard me right. We haven't been formally introduced, so let me introduce myself. I'm your older brother Marco, and I'm ready to take what's mines "

Chapter 1

Chance:

I couldn't believe my brother, that I just recently found out I had, had me tied up like I was some fucking animal. When I found out about him, I thought I would find him and build some type of bond, but this nigga had taken shit to a whole new level. The fact that he caught me slipping is what was pissing me off the most. Not to mention, my newborn and future wife were probably worried sick. I knew Dior was pissed because she had been calling a nigga's phone non-stop for the past three days. I had to get the fuck up out of here, but I wasn't going to let him see me sweat.

"Ok, so you're my older brother, but what the fuck do you want from me?"

"I'm coming to take over and I know a nigga like you will not give up your spot easily, so I'm willing to take it to the next level if need be. You see my man, I thought about taking the easy route and talking to you about getting this bread together, but I had been following you around and I see you not an easy dude to break. This shit is more of a personal matter than anything though."

"Personal? Nigga I don't even know you, so how is it personal? Fuck all that my man. We can make this shit an easy situation and you can let me go, or we can do shit the hard way." He started smiling.

"I don't think you are in the position to be making threats nigga, so I advise you to think before you speak. This shit personal because you've always been the nigga that got what he wanted. All I ever wanted Pops to do was show me the same love he showed you, but the nigga was so stuck up in you and your mother's ass he couldn't see anything else. He went back and forth from your mother to mine, breaking my mother down each time because she knew he wasn't happy when it came to her. The fact that your mother gave him an ultimatum of being with her or my mother and he just left us to struggle and make it on our own is what made me hate you even more. I let the shit go and accepted the fact that I was another nigga that was growing up without a father, until I saw how lavish the nigga had y'all living. I would never understand how a man could just leave his responsibility for a bitch."

"Yo, my mans," I cut him off. "I understand you in your little feelings and all, but my mother will not be too many more bitches. Now, the fact that you placing blame on the next man for what our father did shows just how pussy you are." He punched me in the face and I smirked, while spitting my blood on him. I didn't know what type of nigga he thought I was, but I wasn't the type of nigga that folds under pressure.

"You got a lot of heart. I respect that, but that heart won't get you out of here alive. I don't play games and I damn sure don't care if I have to kill you to stake my claim. Let me put you on game a lil bit baby bro."

"What the fuck are you talking about? I don't need a bitch nigga to put me up on shit. Untie me right now nigga."

"You want to know what's crazy? I killed Pops' bitch ass. That nigga didn't mean shit to me. I would do it again if I could. So if I were you I word watch my words. I hated the way he showed favoritism to you and your hoe ass sisters. Do you know what I went through all my life? I lived off hand me downs, the government, and my mother turning to drugs because she was depressed over him. So yeah, I killed that nigga."

"So you killed your mother too, right? Nigga, you have to be a real ain't shit nigga to kill the man that gave you life. Real shit nigga, if I get out of this shit, you dead nigga, brother or not." I was livid. I have been trying to kill a nigga that had nothing to do with my pops' murder, when it was his own child that took his life from him. This is all fucked up. Now I have to figure out how to get out of this bullshit. This nigga has to go. And to think, I was going to try to reconcile with this snake. I was so caught up in my thoughts that I didn't even see the nigga had two bodies lying on the floor next to me. This clown was a dead man walking.

4

"I didn't kill my mother, your mother had her killed. You think she is so innocent, but nigga, your life is one big lie. She is nothing but a snake her damn self. But don't worry, her time is coming soon. You will find out she is not who she claims to be. I bet she's still kicking that lie to you like she is still running shit in New York, huh?" I wanted to know where he was going with this. I was pissed, but I wouldn't let it show.

I laughed and smirked because he thought this shit was some type of game. "Don't even think about touching my mother. You playing a real dangerous game Marco, and it won't end well. What, you thought these bodies down here would intimidate me? I'm not no scary ass nigga."

"Speaking of these bodies, I heard your baby's mother been missing," he kicked the body over and it was Moe, that crushed a nigga something serious. I couldn't believe he did this to my baby mama. From where I was, I could see that she wasn't dead, but death would become of her soon. I had to get us out of here. He turned the other body over and it was Drake, now I was all confused.

"What did they have to do with this?" How did he even know who they were? And furthermore, what were they doing here together?

"Babyboy, I see you not smart at all. You thought you had you a loyal hoe, huh? Well, this bitch is far from it. I had her set this nigga up and she failed because she couldn't keep them hoe ass legs closed. Everybody around me thinks I'm something to play with, but you and them niggas will learn today. I moved here two years ago, watching every move you made, and I knew I had to come up with something. This nigga Drake was always at his mom's crib, so I got myself acquainted. He introduced me to that bitch Cody and the rest was history. I set it all up so that you two would kill each other and I'd come out on top, smart right?"

"You a real slick, snake ass nigga." He was really pissing me off with all this bitching. It took me a minute to recognize that the two dudes that were standing here were the same dudes from the club with Trey.

"So that's how y'all niggas get down? Y'all mad because of a punk ass argument at a club, so y'all team up with this nigga to kill me? I started laughing because I couldn't take these niggas serious. "A click full of pussies." Marco hit me across the nose with the butt of his gun. When I got loose, it would be hell to pay.

Dior:

I don't know whether to cry or be pissed. I have been calling Chance for the past three days and not getting an answer. This is not like him at all, so I was starting to get worried. His ass better not be with a bitch, I know that much. When he didn't come home the other night after he told me to get dressed for a romantic night out, I drove around to different places he usually hangs, but everybody was saying they hadn't seen him. My phone started ringing and I answered without looking at the screen.

"HELLO!" I was frustrated beyond the max.

"What up sis, you busy?"

"No, just frustrated as hell. What's up bro, you good?"

"Hell yeah. I'm out man, come scoop me."

"I'm on the way." My anger faded away partially because my brother was finally able to come home. I don't know how the hell he got out with all the charges he had, but I would worry about it some other time. I ran upstairs and threw on a Nike suit with a pair of Air Max. I grabbed Cayleigh an outfit to throw on right quick since we were coming back home. My hair was in faux locs, so I didn't have to worry about that. I packed Cayleigh's bag and we headed out. On the way to the jail, I called Chance four more times and got the same results. A bitch was livid now because this nigga had some nerve to leave me with a newborn and not return my calls. I have never been the type to be insecure, but he was leaving me no choice. I pulled up at the Fulton County Jail and waited about fifteen minutes for Dakota to come out. My brother looked horrible. The first place I would be taking him was to the barbershop. He got in the backseat with Cayleigh and tried to pick her up, until I stopped him.

"No deal nigga. You stink and probably got bed bugs and shit on you. I know this your first time seeing her, but you're off limits until you wash your sweaty ass and musty balls."

"Shitttt, ain't nothing musty about these balls, you tripping. What's up though, why you acting all salty?"

"Something is going on with Chance bro. I know you probably don't want to hear about him, but I'm worried and I kind of need your help. I will see if Jas will watch Cayleigh for a while, but I need you to help me find him. Do this for me, please. I have nobody else."

"I don't know sis. You know what me and this nigga got going on, that's asking a lot." I understood where he was coming from, but for the moment, I wished he would put that to the side. We pulled up to the barbershop and I waited outside for him to come out. While waiting, I called Jas to see if she would watch Cayleigh for a while.

"Well look at God. If it isn't my disappearing ass best friend."

"Hey Jas, you busy? I need a huge favor."

"What's up bitch?"

"I have to find Chance. I'm worried sick about him, so I need you to watch Cayleigh for a few hours."

"You know I got you boo. Is everything alright?"

"To be honest, I'm not sure. I can only hope so. I will be on my way in a few. And Jas, Dakota is with me, so don't be on no bull."

"Oh shit, when did his stupid ass get out? Never mind, it's not even important, I will see you in a few." Jas was a damn mess; I knew they were about to be on some bullshit.

"Alright bitch."

Dakota finally came out and he was looking like he had something to tell me.

"You not going to believe this shit."

"What nigga? Stop playing."

"Come to find out, that nigga King comes here to get his haircut. Chuck says King was in here the other day."

"What the fuck Dakota? That's some whack ass information. How the fuck is that going to help me?" I didn't mean to click like that, but my brother was pissing me off.

"Got damn Dior, let a nigga finish before you start talking shit. He says King found out Moe was still alive and rushed out of the shop. While he was walking to his car, some niggas jacked him and threw him in a white van." My heart started beating out of my chest, what if they hurt him?

"Oh my God. Cody, we have to find him. So them niggas just stood there and watched while he got snatched up? What type of shit is that? He could be hurt. How is Moe alive? Where is Drake?" I was panicking, how could all of this be? There were so many questions and nobody had the answers to them. I sped off from the shop, headed to Jas' house. Somebody had some explaining to do and shit was about to get real.

"Yo, what kind of phone that nigga got sis?"

"We both have the iPhone 6 plus, why? What the fuck does that have to do with anything?"

"Aye, I know you mad, but pipe the fuck down. Don't y'all females be putting that Find My iPhone shit on y'all nigga's phone when you think he cheating? Maybe we can find the nigga that way."

"I didn't put it on his phone Cody. I never thought he was cheating because he never gave me a reason to believe he was. I will try it though and see what comes up." We pulled up at Jas' house and she was standing outside with her hands folded across her chest. Her little stomach was starting to show and it was too cute.

"What's up Jas? You couldn't answer a nigga's calls while he was jammed up?" Jas cocked her head to the side and rolled her eyes.

"Nigga, I am not your bitch, so don't come over here trying to check me. I didn't answer because we had nothing to talk about. You chose who you wanted to be with, so you should have been calling that hoe. Dior, give me my baby so you can get him out of my face please."

"So you trying to turn up in front of my sister, right? I'll be back when we get through handling this little business and I bet that attitude better be gone, with your stankin ass. Let's go Dior, before I do something to her stupid ass." He stormed off and got in the car.

"Alright, I'll be back to get her as soon as I find out something." I wasn't worried about what they had going on because I was used to Cody and his drama, but for now, I was worried about getting my baby back.

Chapter 2

Cody:

I was too happy to be free, even though I wasn't in there long. The fact that I was even in the presence of those pigs had me fucked up, especially the fact that I was missing money. The part that pisses me off more is that they didn't even give me all of my property back, and the biggest lost was my seventy-five thousand dollar Audemar Rolex. I'm not sweating that little shit though. It was just a minor setback for a major comeback. Dior really fucked a nigga up when she asked me to find her little sweet ass boyfriend, knowing damn well we don't fuck with each other, so you know it had to be the love I have for her. I just hope her ass didn't take this shit as me reconciling with this nigga. Jas trying to play that hard shit like she doesn't miss a nigga and shit, when I could tell she wanted to fuck right then and there.

"Aye sis, did you tell Jas I was with you?"

"Yeah, why?" That was my verification that she wanted this dick and I would be back to give it to her.

"No reason. So did you download the app like I said? We need to make this as quick as possible. You know I'm really not feeling this shit anyway." She looked at me out of the corner of her eyes and I knew she was about to pop off.

"No, I did not download it and you can shut the hell up whining. You can do me this one favor without bitching because I'm really not in the mood. Either you shut up or I can do this on my own." I sure didn't miss this smart ass mouth. She continued to bitch, so I tuned her out and shot Bree a text, letting her know Daddy was home.

Me: Just letting you know I'm out and I missed you.

A text came back immediately, basically letting me know her stupid ass still had me on block. This was the childish shit I was talking about. I would just stop by her house when I got the chance. I had not one, but two stupid ass baby mamas that I had to put in check. These bitches were getting out of hand. It was either that, or beat both of their ass. I refuse to be one of those niggas that let his baby mamas run over him because they scared of child support.

"Aye Dior, I need to stop by the crib to change and grab Nina and Carol." Nina was my Desert Eagle and Carol was my AK 47. I never did dirty work without my two main bitches. We pulled up to my condo at the Twelve so that I could get all my shit together. Dior sat on the couch, as I went to hop in the shower and get dressed. I jumped out, threw on a pair of black Robin's Jeans, a black and gold hoodie with a pair of black Timbs. I didn't put on any jewelry since I didn't know what we were about to get into. I grabbed Nina and Carol, then headed towards the living room.

"Alright Dior, let's bounce."

"About time nigga. You take longer than I do getting dressed. I got the address to where he is supposed to be, this Find My iPhone app ain't no joke."

"We can take one of my whips."

We got into my black on black Camaro, she plugged the address into the GPS and we took off. I'm happy I always made sure my sister went to the gun range at least twice a week, in case she needed to protect herself. I just hope shit didn't go left. I really didn't want her doing this type of shit, but I know she has her mind made up and ain't no changing it. Dior pulled out her pink diamond encrusted 9mm Luger and loaded up. I swear she thought she was one of them *Gang of Roses* bitches. I've never seen a female that wasn't scared of shit like this, but I had to give it to her, my sister was a true rider. We pulled up in Roswell, where the address said Chance would be, and I parked down the block. There were two cars in the driveway, the van that they said King was thrown into, and a clean ass white on white Aston Martin. We sat there, scoping the scene for about an hour, just to see if anybody would come out or go in before we got out of the car.

"Ok sis, we have done shit like this many times before. We going through the back door. I'm going to pick the locks and go in first, understood?"

"Yeah, I got you, let's get my baby." I couldn't believe she was really sprung over this nigga. That shit made me sick to my stomach. I picked the back lock and to my surprise, the door was already unlocked. We crept in and heard talking in the living room. I was not ready for what was in front of me.

"MARCO, what the fuck? So this where you've been hiding?" I had Carol pointed dead at his head and Dior had Brittany focused on the two niggas he was talking to. This nigga been on some snake shit and he was about to pay for it. I didn't deal with disloyalty too well.

King:

I was in and out of it, due to Marco hitting me in the head with his gun repeatedly. I was sure my nose and jaw were broken, but that didn't matter because I was still trying to find a way out of here. I heard a lot of commotion going on upstairs and I could have sworn I heard the nigga Cody talking, but I knew I was tripping and it wasn't him because he was still locked up. I looked on the floor and Moe looked like she was giving up at any moment. The voices sounded as if they were getting closer.

"Nigga, you brought this bitch of a sister in here, knowing she ain't gone shoot shit. I didn't think you were this fucking dumb man." Dior cocked her head to the side and shot him in the hand. He lost balance, then fell down the stairs from the pain.

"You a snake nigga. Snakes don't live long my nigga, what the fuck you on? I fed you nigga, you supposed to be my right hand." I heard more feet coming down the steps. I opened my eyes as best as I could.

"You fed me? You and Drake were splitting the money evenly and giving me what was left, that's not eating my niggas, that's getting played. Y'all were playing me like I was a corner boy or some shit."

"Dior, what the fuck?" I couldn't figure out what the fuck my future wife was doing here and furthermore, what the fuck was Cody doing here? I know she didn't betray me like this. "My mother told me not to trust you, so this how it's gone be? You working with this nigga?" I was so fucked up that I didn't even see the actual situation that was in front of me. I didn't see that Dior and Cody had guns pointed at Marco and his two do boys. She glanced at me, then trained her eyes back on the niggas in front of her.

"Chance, what the hell are you talking about? We came to get you so all that shit you talking, you can really kill it. How the fuck did you even get yourself in this situation?"

"Shut the fuck up," Marco yelled, causing everyone to look his way. "Cody, my man, you couldn't have possibly thought I would work under you forever. You treated me like I was some corner boy and I am not that nigga. I've been plotting on taking you out for quite some time."

"What the fuck you talking about nigga? You ate just as much as I ate, I never fed you crumbs. So this what all this shit about? That's between me and you, what the fuck this nigga got to do with it?" he said as he pointed towards me.

"That whole bitch over there happens to be my little brother." Cody and Dior's face hit the floor as they took on the news. Dior's eyes welled up with tears and my heart crushed seeing her in this state and there was nothing I could do. How did they even find out where I was? This was not adding up at all. Cody looked toward the floor and his face was that of rage.

"Yo, how the fuck could you do all this? How could you kill Drake? Nigga, you real foul for this shit." He walked closer to Marco and before he could respond, Cody shot Marco twice in both legs and kneeled beside him. "If it's one thing you always knew about me, it's that I would kill, no questions asked, about my family. He stood up and shot him right in the neck. He looked at Nard and Reese and was about to shoot.

"Yo, let me get at them niggas my man." He looked at me with a scowl on his face, as Dior ran over to me and rubbed all over my face.

"Baby, are you ok? Let me get you loose." She started tugging at the rope, then realized it was too tight. She ran upstairs to get something to cut me loose, as Cody just stood there with his gun still trained on the two dudes.

"Aye, isn't that your baby moms? Is she dead or nah?" This nigga was cracking jokes like this situation was funny.

"Nigga, ain't nothing joke mode about this shit, so you can stop laughing, real spit."

"You talking with your chest out like one of these bullets can't bless you or something. Watch your fucking mouth playboy. This here is my bitch boy gun, and you the main bitch boy it's been looking for, but Dior sparing you, so keep quiet nigga." He never took his eyes off the main target as he spoke. Dior came over and started cutting on the rope.

"What the fuck? Is that Moe?" she ran over to Moe and checked her pulse. Moe was a strong ass woman to still be fighting this hard. We have to get her to a hospital.

"So you two niggas were going to help this nigga kill me, right?"

"Yo fam, I told this nigga not to do this shit. I knew this was a bad idea," Nard said.

I took Dior's gun, then trained it on Nard's head, shooting him in between the eyes. Reese was trying to plead his case. I walked up to him and placed it against his temple, "I'm not y'all fam." I shot him and his brain matter painted my face. Cody stood there with a smirk on his face and with venom in his eyes. I hate I had to apologize to this nigga, but right now wasn't the time. I ran over to Moe and scooped her up, ready to go, but Cody stood there, staring at his homie Drake.

"I can't believe he killed my mans. What the fuck I'm supposed to do now?"

"We have to get out of here. I will explain everything, but we have to get out of here. I'm pretty sure 12 headed this way."

Dior grabbed her brother by the arm and we ran out. I couldn't believe we were in each other's presence and haven't killed one another yet.

"Hold on Moe, just hold on." I can't believe all this happened. Here I was, raising my son alone, thinking his mother was dead, but she was alive the whole time. How the fuck was I going to explain this to Christian? Dior hasn't said much at all, which is weird, considering the fact she hasn't seen me, so I thought she would be happier than she was.

"Babe, you aight, why you so quiet?"

"No, I am not. Can you explain this shit to me? Can you explain how the fuck you ended up kidnapped with a bitch that was said to be dead damn near a year ago? When you can explain that shit, we will talk."

"Wait a fucking minute. You not worried about the fact that I could be dead right now, but your dumb ass worried about why I was around Moe. Yo, you can't be fucking serious, you sound dumb ass fuck."

"Yo, Chance, is it?" he was looking at me through the rearview. "I understand shit seems a little fucked up for you, but watch your mouth when you talking to my sister. You still not exempt from catching a bullet, keep that in mind. I still have two in the chamber and we can get it popping."

"Fuck all that my nigga. You been talking real tough, but ain't intimidated me a bit. You ain't shot shit and you not going to, so dead all that rah rah shit."

"No deal. You two will not do this shit right now, chill the fuck out. Chance, we will discuss this when we get to this hospital. I don't have time for y'all bullshit." We both looked at Dior like she was out of her mind. I don't know who the hell she thought she was talking to. It took us all of fifteen minutes to get to Grady. We passed another hospital, but Grady had the best trauma center. I ran inside to grab some of the nurses and a stretcher, then they rushed Moe to the back. I was still in shock because for the past nine months, Moe was assumed to be dead and I was still shocked. If she had been with Marco for all this time and just left Christian, she will be getting chumped off. I saw Dior headed my way and shook my head because I knew she was about to act stupid.

"So, do you mind informing me on how your black ass ended up with Moe, and don't even think about telling a lie. Help me understand how her dusty ass ended up still being alive and Drake being dead." She was laying the questions on me heavy, but it was too much to talk about in front of all these people in this waiting room. People were already being nosey and shit.

"Yo, what the fuck y'all looking at? We not giving y'all nosey asses a show. Turn y'all got damn heads before I air this bitch out."

"Bring your ass outside. You tripping, got these motherfuckers watching me and shit. You know I don't even get down like that." I grabbed her by the arm and we headed outside.

She snatched her arm away from me, "Ok nigga, start talking."

I told her everything from Marco being my brother, to him being the person behind me and her brother's beef. It was hard to accept that he killed his own pops. I was more so hurt that I couldn't build some type of bond with him because he had a different motive in mind. She shook her head in disbelief of the whole situation.

"I can't believe Marco was a snake after the bond him and Cody had. I can't imagine how my brother feels knowing that his right hand man killed his other one. I always felt like he was the jealous type though."

"Now how the fuck did you find me, and furthermore, what the fuck were you doing putting yourself in danger like that? Come on ma, I'm a grown ass man, I don't need you coming to my rescue. What would have happened if we were both killed? Who would take care of Cayleigh and Christian? You have to be smart and make better decisions." She looked at me with a scowl on her face, but I didn't give a damn, I was speaking facts.

"You are one ungrateful ass nigga. If you haven't figured the shit out by now, you will. I ride for mine Mr. McCray, all day, and will die for mine. You may feel I wasn't being smart, but if you must know, I've been doing this shit, this ain't nothing new to me. I could probably shoot the heat better than you." With that being said, she walked off. This conversation was not over, she will explain just what she meant eventually. No lady of mine was about to be out shooting motherfuckers like it was *Call of Duty*.

I walked back in and sat next to Dior, while her brother sat on the other side of the room. I still hated the fact that eventually I would have to talk to him about my brother and apologize. I didn't know how that would turn out, knowing how fucked up his mouth was, and mine wasn't the best either. "You can go pick up Cayleigh and head home, I'll be home in a few." She started laughing hysterically.

"Nigga, you got me fucked up. What I look like leaving my nigga with his baby mama that still wants him? Ain't no rekindled flames bih. I'm going to sit my fine thick ass right here until you ready. On her death bed or not, I don't trust that bitch." Dior didn't know how bad she was pissing me off with all this extra shit, especially when she walked off like she had an attitude earlier and didn't elaborate on what she meant.

"Dior, you acting real aggy right about now. What the fuck can she fucking do to me? Grow up ma, that childish shit not a good look on you."

"Family of Monique Baker?" I never paid attention to the fact they had the same name until now, since I knew they were sisters. It was just my luck to be the nigga that had two sisters dick crazy.

"What's up doc, how is she?"

"Well as you know, she lost a tremendous amount of blood from sitting so long, but she is a fighter. We removed one of the bullets, but the other bullet is extremely close to a major organ. We gave her two blood transfusions, but I'm sorry to tell you that she slipped into a coma. We will continue doing all we can, but due to these circumstances, we can't promise she will make it."

I heard everything the doctor said, but I was spaced out from everything. Here I was, raising my son alone for almost a year, thinking his mother was dead. Then being kidnapped by my own blood and finding her barely alive, only to be told she still might die. This shit was stressing me out and I felt myself about to spaz at any moment. I had to get myself together. I was so caught up, worried about Moe, that I didn't realize I needed to be seen my damn self. I was certain my nose and jaw were broken, not to mention, I still wasn't completely healed from when I was shot. I walked over to the nurses' station and checked myself in. I knew I was about to be here all night.

Chapter 3

Dior:

Chance had to be a damn fool to ask me to leave him here with that bitch. This entire situation had my head hurting because I knew something was not right. How does Moe end up with Marco and how does Drake end up dead? It hurt me to the core when I saw Drake laid there, lifeless. Yes, he got on my last nerve, but that was my first everything, so of course it did something to me. Chance thought I put myself in danger, but like I told him, I've been doing this shit.

Four years ago:

It was lunch time and I was starving, so I would stay in today, instead of going to the courtyard. I saw Dakota and Drake sitting on the other side, waiting on me to come over. I had a taste for wings today so I got a five piece wing with fries and made my way to where they were. I went over and sat on Drake's lap, as I always did.

"What's up sis? We got a proposition for you, if you ready for this life like you say and you're ready to get paid."

"What we talking about?"

"It's a nigga name Cole that just started school here and they say his pops caked up on cash. You need to get to know him and you know the rest." Now usually Drake wasn't with the idea of me doing these types of things, but I've been getting on his nerves about helping and making my own money. They had been robbing niggas and selling work ever since my mother left. Twice a week, we go to the gun range and your girl here had mad skills. I started talking to Cole and over a period of time, we built a small bond. I actually grew feelings for him, but I loved Drake more. One weekend his parents went out of town and I made my move. I fucked him until he was out of it. When he woke up, he was staring down the barrel of my chromed out .380. While he was sleeping, I had already screwed the silencer on. I made him show me where his dad kept most of his money and jewelry, then shot him right in

between the eyes. I wiped everything down with bleach, cleaned his dick off to remove any of my DNA and left like I was never there. I was paid a hundred and sixty thousand dollars and from that day forward, I was in love with it. I was only 17 when I entered that life. Every week I had different jobs that I was in charge of completing, making anywhere from a hundred and sixty to two hundred and fifty thousand dollars. I was a paid bitch by the time I was legal.

"Hello, Dior, can you fucking hear?" I completely forgot Dakota was with us since he was all distant and what not.

"What?"

"I said are you ready to go? I got some shit I need to handle and I'm not sitting here with you and your little boyfriend all night. This ain't got shit to do with me." I was so sick of Dakota whining about nothing. "You can go ahead and leave, I will call Uber to get to my car from your spot."

"Alright sis, be safe." Chance went up to see Moe, so I went to the nurses' station to get her room info. When I reached the fourth floor, Chance was talking to the doctor, so I stood off to the side and waited for them to finish talking.

"I don't know if you were aware of Ms. Baker's pregnancy, but of course the fetus didn't survive, due to such trauma. We are working extremely hard to keep her alive, but I will be honest, it's not looking too good."

"Pregnant? How far along was she?" Chance didn't see me standing where I was, but he looked as if he was very concerned. I also felt a bit of sympathy for her. Even though we had our differences, I wouldn't wish losing a child on anyone.

"From the tests we ran, we calculated she was an estimated twelve weeks." I couldn't believe Marco tried to kill somebody with child, possibly his child at that. How could he be so heartless? I wonder was she pregnant by him though. The doctor walked off as I walked over to where Chance was standing.

"Hey, what are they saying?" He shook his head and started walking off.

"Damn Chance, I apologize for the way I acted back there, but you have to put yourself in my shoes and understand all of this caught me off guard." Chance looked at me with the most disgusted face.

"Dior, you sound very childish right now and I thought I asked you to leave. I don't have time for this right now, just go get my daughter and take your ass home." He started walking off and I followed right behind him. There was no way in hell he was talking to me like I was some random.

"Oh hell no, Cayleigh is fine. Yes, you told me to go home and I told your ass no. You can call me what you want, but what you won't do is push me out when I'm only trying to be here for you. I am tired of you always pushing me out all the time. You're just like all the rest of these selfish ass niggas."

He stopped in his tracks and turned facing me, "If that's how you feel ma, you can kick rocks because I didn't ask your little spoiled ass for your help me anyway. You kicking that rah rah shit like you really trying to be here for a nigga, when you know you really only here because you don't want me around my baby mama. Grow up ma. I don't want Moe, but what I won't do is leave her here all alone when I'm all she has. What type of nigga you take me for? You really need to grow up Dior." I felt the tears building up, but I'll be damn if I let them fall.

"You're absolutely right. I will most certainly kick rocks nigga. Fuck you Chance. You haven't been home, nor seen your daughter, but you want to sit your black ass in this hospital like we don't matter, for a bitch that played dead and left you to take care of her son. You not even worried about the fact that your face all fucked up, all you worried about is Moe. It's all good you ungrateful ass bastard. A real nigga would salute his lady for riding for him, but your lame ass is mad, so cool, I will leave." He had me fucked up. I turned to leave and the tears started falling. I go hard to get my man back and he gets mad at me for looking out. I called Jas to come get me and she was on the way. I couldn't believe Chance piped up on me the way he did.

Bree:

This pregnancy has been the absolute worst. I thought morning sickness only lasted the first trimester, but here I was, seven damn months and sick as a dog. Rashad was released this morning and said he would be by later. I knew it would only be a matter of time before Dakota was released as well. My older sister Adore was in town from New Orleans, so I was getting dressed to hang with her for a while. Adore was twenty-four years old and beautiful as hell. She was 5'6, 32D breasts, mocha brown complexion, like me, with a size sixteen waist. My sister was what some would call a BBW, but that took nothing away from her beauty. Adore's hair stopped in the middle of her back and she always wore it bone straight with red streaks that complemented her big brown eyes. I couldn't even lie, my sister was bad. I put on my neon green PINK outfit, with a pair of Ugg boots so that I would be comfortable. I fixed my hair in a messy bun and pulled out a few strands to cradle my face. I sprayed on my Coco Chanel fragrance, grabbed my MK bag and headed out the door. I shot Adore a text, letting her know I was on the way and to be ready. She was the slowest person when it came to getting dressed. My phone started ringing and it was a number I have never seen before, so I hit ignore really quick, without thinking twice. Whoever it was, called right back, and this time I answered.

"Who is this?"

"What's up baby? Daddy's home."

"Who daddy? What do you want Dakota? I'm busy." I could not believe he was calling me. I can't lie, his voice sounded so sexy and made a bitch very horny. I haven't had sex in months and Rashad can't get the cookies because I'm pregnant by Dakota and I'm not trifling. I have done some shit in my days, but that would never be one of them. Baby daddy might get lucky tonight.

"I need to see you, where you at?"

"My sister is in town so I'm about to kick it with her for a minute. What you want to see me for because you not getting no ass." I knew damn well I was lying because he was getting this ass tonight and I will hate him again when we were done.

"Girl please, if I wanted that ass, I would get it. That's always going to be me. I know that Pookie looking ass nigga ain't doing nothing for you." I had tears in my eyes from laughing at his stupid ass.

"You so petty Dakota. Why you have to call that man Pookie, he looks better than you." Lies, all lies. Rashad wasn't touching Cody on any level, but I would never tell him that. "Call me about 9, I should be home by then."

"Bet. Make sure that thang shaved and warm for me." Now, I know y'all probably like this bitch stupid. Hell, I'm saying the same thing, but I'm horny as hell and nobody puts it down like baby daddy. I pulled up to the Westin Hotel downtown, where my sister was staying. I don't know why she chose to stay here when I had a whole house to myself. Adore came out and got in the car, smiling hard as hell.

"Bih, you must have got you some, you all happy and everything. What's up bih, give me a hug." I haven't seen my sister since my high school graduation and I missed her so much. We have the best bond anybody could ask for.

"So what's been up little sis, you all pregnant and what not. You think you grown busting that thang open and shit. I can't wait to meet the man in your life and make sure I approve."

"We not together anymore, E. He plays too many games for me." She twisted up her face at me. Me and E were two peas in a pod, but we were the complete opposite of one another. While I have always been the loving and affectionate one, she could care less about love and a nigga's feelings. I fell in love with every damn body, I was so weak for a nigga. All he needed was a good third leg and I was sold, sad to say. I never understood how she could just cut her feelings off the way she does and not worry about anything.

"Games? That's all these niggas good for sis. I have told you on numerous occasions you can't trust they ass as far as you can throw them. You can't be so quick to fall in love and give your all when they're only going to give you what they want you to have. Cortez is the exact reason I don't trust these niggas now." Cortez was my sister's ex- boyfriend that she was with for seven years, and a true ain't shit nigga he was. My sister got pregnant and he straight dissed her and ruined her name in the streets, so if it's anybody that has been threw shit with a nigga, it was E. We stayed out until about seven and I went home to get ready for Dakota to come give my kitty some TLC. I pulled up at my house and ran in to take a shower before it was time for him to arrive. I washed my body down with Victoria's Secret Pure Seduction body wash and lotioned my body down with the Seduction lotion. I knew what my plans were, so I threw on a wife beater with no panties under it. I couldn't stop laughing at how big my stomach was and how I couldn't see my feet. I felt like a fool for the move I was about to make after how Dakota acted, but Rashad wasn't tapping this ass anytime soon. The fact that he didn't show up nor call made the situation so much easier. I heard someone at the door and I knew without a doubt that it was Dakota, so I went downstairs to open the door.

"What's up, Ms. Bree? Damn, it's like that ma? You come to the door like that, huh? You ready to bust it open for a real nigga." I swear he makes my ass itch because he has no sense. I don't know what he was on, but I wasn't trying to play any games. I wanted to get my rocks off with no strings attached.

"You know why you came over here baby daddy, let's not play stupid. I know what you want and I want it too. I started unzipping his pants, while kissing on his neck and his dick started rising immediately. I pulled his pants down, then pushed him on the couch and straddled him. Sliding down slowly, I felt my cat throbbing, as my juices started flowing rapidly.

"Sss, mm," I was biting down on my bottom lip as I started riding him slowly.

"Fuck, this pussy feels good bae. You tight as hell." Dakota started matching my rhythm and grinding from below as I reached my first peak.

"Ahh, I'm about to cum daddy. It feels so good."

"Get on your knees." I did as I was told, arching my back as best as I could with this big ass stomach. I closed my eyes as I waited for him to enter and beat my insides out. He rammed in my tunnel, causing me to squirt on impact. He started teasing my opening, going in and out with only the head.

"Oh my God, daddy, it feels so good. I'm cumin." Dakota was hitting my walls and attacking my g-spot.

"Shit," he was groaning and moaning while I threw my ass back, each time he pumped.

"Fuck, I'm about to bust. Cum one more time for me ma." He picked up his pace, showing my kitty no mercy. We came in unison and within five minutes of our make-up session, we were knocked out.

Chapter 4

Cody:

I sure had a hell of a welcome home party. I couldn't believe I went along with Dior's retarded ass, playing Captain Planet and shit, trying to save the world. A nigga would have never guessed Marco was plotting on a nigga, but then again, I should have known because of the way he was acting. I was still in the dark about why he was trying to kill Chance, and more so how the fuck they ended up being brothers. The fact that Moe was alive and my right hand Drake was gone, had my mental all twisted up. I had a hell of a day, but my night ended on a good note, Bree put it on a nigga. I ain't never tapped out. I was coming over to talk, but it seems like her horny ass had different plans for a nigga. I woke up the next morning, ready for round two, I had to redeem myself. She was still sleep, so I slid my head under the cover, ready to devour the cat for breakfast.

"Mm," she started waking up out of her sleep. I started sucking the clit as if I was sucking a pacifier, then started slurping on it. I stuck two fingers inside of her tunnel, while making each letter of the alphabet with my tongue, backwards. "Right there baby, don't stop."

"Mm ma, you taste so good. Daddy making Ms. Kitty feel good?"

"Yes, ahh." Her eyes were rolling to the back of her head as I felt her body tense up and her legs start shaking. "I'm about to cum."

I picked up the pace of my tongue, sticking it in and out, tongue fucking her and vibrating my tongue as I slowed down. "You going to stop tripping on a nigga?" She didn't answer, so I stopped.

"Dakota, stop playing, keep going."

"Nope, I asked you a question." She looked like she was about to say something, so I stuck my tongue back in, then started nibbling on her clit, and her words got caught in her throat. "Are you going to stop tripping on a nigga?" I jumped up and stuck the head in and started pounding the pussy. I was being cautious not to hurt my babies, but I was showing the cat no mercy.

"Yes, I 'ma be good baby. Yes, right there."

"Argh," Bree had me in here moaning and grunting like a bitch. I threw both of her legs on my shoulders and started slow grinding, making sure I hit every nook and cranny of her walls.

"Ooh, it feels…sooo…good."

"You missed this dick ma? Fuck, argh."

"Yes, I missed it. Go harder please."

"What's my name? Spell it for me ma," I whispered in her ear and started sucking on her nipples. I was praying no milk came out, but I was so deep in it, I wouldn't have given a fuck.

"Daddy-A-K-K-K," I started going harder and she started stuttering.

"I'm about to bust ma," I picked up my pace. SMACK, I smacked her on the ass. Her legs started shaking. SMACK. "I'm cumin." I shot a huge ass load inside of her. I'm happy she was already pregnant. I jumped up and went to take a shower. She came and jumped in the shower with me and we washed each other off. I washed Bree down and massaged her shoulders, taking my precious time with her. She returned the favor, then we hopped out. I had some business to handle, so I got dressed to head out. I threw on a pair of Robin's jeans with a Versace hoodie, and a pair of Prada's. I had to go home first to cop some jewelry to put on because a nigga felt naked without it.

"Yo ma, I'll be back later. I got some business to handle, but we still need to talk."

"About?"

"Just be ready when I get back Bree." I walked over, gave her a kiss, and dipped. I was going to get my shorty back, whether she liked it or not, that pussy had my name stamped on that.

King:

I was watching the news and saw that they found three male bodies at a house in Roswell. I knew it was Marco and his bitch boys, and I didn't feel an ounce of remorse about it. I would do the shit over and over again because that's what happens when you don't know who you fucking with, so fuck him and them niggas. I didn't mean to go off on my baby the way I did, but she was killing me with that insecure, spoiled shit. I'm the nigga that's been kidnapped and shit, but she acting like it didn't mean shit. On top of that, my baby mama ended up being alive, so she was supposed to understand my reason of wanting to be here. Dior thought I was trying to get back with Moe, but that was far from the truth. This bitch had a lot of explaining to do if and when she did wake up. The situation with Marco was really fucking with me. I needed to go see my mother and see what else she's been keeping from me because this shit was not adding up. I shot my baby a text to apologize and try to make amends.

Me: I'm sorry bae, we good?

Wifey: Nope, you have to work for it. You really tried me, Mr. McCray. Goodnight, enjoy your night with your first lady.

Me: You tripping, but I'm not kissing your ass ma. Be easy.

I meant every word of it too. I wasn't about to kiss her spoiled ass. Not today, not ever. I left the hospital, in route to my mother's house. I pulled up to Madukes' crib and there were two cars in the driveway. *Who the fuck she got over here now?* I walked in to the aroma of fried chicken, collard greens, macaroni and cheese, and cornbread. Madukes in the kitchen whipping up a meal like it was Thanksgiving. She had the music so loud that she didn't even hear me come in, so I walked towards the den and both of my sisters were sitting in there with some little young nigga and two little young ass females. I could tell these females were hot in the ass, so they had no business over here with my sisters. My sisters thought they were grown and it pissed me off that my mother allowed it. Cali was nineteen and Chasity was seventeen, but in my eyes, they were still little ass girls.

"What the fuck is this?"

"Hey, big bro." They both looked at me and gave me that please don't embarrass me look.

"Aye nigga, who are you?" I wasn't in the mood to play games with their ass.

"Chance, don't come in here questioning nobody like you run shit." Cali had the big balls and she knew I was about to turn up on her fake grown ass. They already knew I didn't play the bar when it came to them. So for them to have a nigga all up in my mom's crib like he paid some bills was a no go with me. He stood up and walked toward me with his hand out.

"What up fam, my name Nyrue, but you can call me Rue." I'm not a friendly nigga, so he could put his hand down, trying to play innocent and shit. I guess he got the clue and put his hand down by his side.

"Alright Rue, who are you to my sister?" Cali came and stood in between us and folded her arms.

"Um, Chance, he is my boyfriend and no you will not question him like you're my daddy. We've been together since I was fifteen and Mommy said he could come over for dinner, so chill out." Cali was about to get her fast ass knocked the fuck out, trying to boss up in front of this cat, and it wasn't going to be a damn thing anybody here could do about it. "Is that right? So you think you old enough to have niggas in your mama's house Cali? And Chasity, you knew about this shit, so let me guess, you got a nigga too?"

"No Chance, chill out. We have company and would appreciate it if you chill with all the questions." The two females were sitting there, lusting over a nigga like he would actually take that route and rock the cradle with their young asses.

"What the fuck y'all looking at?" Now I was livid. "Yo, everybody take your ass home, the party is over. Rue, or whatever your name is, stay away from my sister."

"Oh hell no. Y'all don't have to leave, y'all good. I am grown, so I date who I want." I gave Cali the meanest scowl because she was about to get knocked right off her feet and didn't even know it.

"I'm about to go holla at ma, and by the time I get back, this shit better be cleared out."

I was pissed off like never before. This has been a hell of a week and talking to Madukes was about to make it worse.

"Yo ma, what is a nigga doing up in here? So you just going to let a whole nigga that's probably fucking your daughter, kick it, huh?"

"No the hell you not, piping up in my shit. What the hell is your problem and why does your face look like that?" I completely forgot my face was still a little fucked up, but that's not important right now.

"I met my brother, but I didn't meet him voluntarily. That nigga kidnapped me and beat my ass. What really put the icing on the cake is he told me you had his mother killed and been lying about New York. So give me some light on this situation, and you better not fucking lie."

"I didn't have shit to do with his crackhead ass mama getting killed. That bitch wasn't worth my time, so he can stop with that bullshit ass lie. The secrets I kept from you will remain kept because in life, it's some shit you have to take to your grave to protect those that you love. When I feel like you can handle the truth, I will tell you, and this the last time I want to hear about it. You got some nerve bringing your big head ass up in here, trying to regulate like your shit just all the way right."

"I'm a grown ass man. I can handle anything, but if that's how you feel, fuck it. You got niggas up in here like you running a hotel and shit, then have the nerve to keep secrets and shit. When Chasity and Cali ass pop up pregnant round this bitch, don't fucking call me." Joyce really pissed me off with all this bullshit she had going on, but it's all good, I will find out what I needed to know. What's done in the dark always comes to the light.

Chapter 5

Adore:

I enjoyed hanging with my sister and giving her the rundown on how to treat these niggas. I am her older sister, Adore, and I have had my fair share of heartbreaks and games. I went through years of low self-esteem, thanks to my ex, Cortez. He dragged me through the mud and I haven't trusted a nigga since. I never understood why he just couldn't find a way to love me when I would bring him the moon and the stars. I mean, what nigga wouldn't appreciate a loyal woman with beauty and brains? I'm a bad BBW, but that wasn't enough for him. With thick thighs, a big round ass, and 32D breasts, I will put these skinny bitches to shame. I was 5'6 with the complexion of mocha chocolate. Low self-esteem ruined me for a while, but I was back and popping. I graduated last year from Harvard University with a Masters in Psychology. I came back to Atlanta to work with a patient that requested my services. My sister always talks about how live it was down here since I moved, but I don't see what the hype is about and I have been back almost two weeks. I got up and got my hygiene together so that I could cruise the city and sightsee a little bit. I showered, then put on my red Esteban Cortazar jumpsuit with my Manolo Blahnik heels. I was not a tennis shoe person at all, so sneakers were a negative. My hair was in wand curls, courtesy of Bree's stylist, Peaches. I sprayed my Hermes 24 Faubourg fragrance, then I grabbed my Hermes clutch and exited out of the building. I had already called Uber, so the driver was sitting outside, waiting. I hopped in the car and told him to pull into a gas station so that I could get some cash. I got out of the car, went inside the gas station and locked eyes with the finest man I have seen since I blessed this city. I grabbed my cash, grabbed something to drink, and stepped to the window to make my purchase.

"Aye my man, let me get fifty on pump 6, and add this beautiful lady's purchase to my tab." I turned to face him and what I was about to say got stuck in my throat. His smile was heaven in itself, he was sculpted by the gods. "You can say thank you ma, ain't no need to get nervous and just stare."

"Oh my God, I am so sorry, I don't know what came over me." He smirked at me and rubbed his chin with his head to the side.

"Don't flex ma, I know I'm one sexy ass nigga, I was blessed that way." With that said, he turned to walk out of the store. I had to get his name. I didn't want to seem thirsty, but it was something about him that intrigued me and piqued my interest. I walked out of the store and towards his car, but stopped in my tracks when I saw he had his lady with him. I turned to walk back towards my car and felt someone tap on my shoulder.

"You don't have to turn back ma, that's not my lady."

I blushed at the fact that he chased me down. "Oh ok, I didn't want to be disrespectful at all. I just forgot to say thank you back there. I'm not usually the type to freeze up on my words, but I apologize.

"You good ma, so what's your name anyway?"

"Adore and yours?" He handed me his phone and told me to save my number, and I did just that.

As he was walking off, he turned around and said, "My name is King by the way." With that being said, he pulled off.

Dior:

Things with me and Chance had been getting worse by the day, and I honestly didn't know how much more I could take. It's been a little over a week since everything happened and instead of bonding, we have been silent with one another. When he does come home, he spends time with Cayleigh and Christian, then leaves without saying goodbye or anything. Whether I'm pissed off or not, I still pray for him when he is in those streets because the streets don't love nobody. I know I couldn't deny the fact that I was missing his touch something terrible. I should have just accepted his apology, but no, my selfish ass had to play hard Dior, like always. I was so stuck in my ways to the point I would never own up to my actions and apologize for anything. He knew what type of female he was dealing with from the jump. I heard the alarm chime, meaning Chance had just arrived, so I placed Cayleigh in her room. Christian was already sleeping, so I tucked him in under the covers. My baby girl was getting so big and even more precious than before. She was almost two months. Since she was asleep, I planned on reconciling and calling a truce with my man, we have been mad long enough. I hopped in the shower to relax my mind and prepare myself for whatever it was that would happen. We have been together over a year, but I still get nervous when it's time to talk to him. I got out of the shower, put vanilla oil all over my body and threw on my silk robe. Chance was in the basement, playing his game like always. He didn't even acknowledge me.

"Can we talk Chance?" *Silence.* I know damn well he wasn't ignoring me.

"Hello, do you not hear me talking to you?" *Silence.* I unplugged his game and stood in front of the TV.

"Yo, get your simple ass out the way. I don't have shit to say to you ma. When you stop being so fucking childish, then we can talk." I didn't know who the fuck he was talking to, but he had the right bitch. I took his game controller and launched it towards his head, hitting him right by his ear.

"Bitch, have you lost your fucking mind? Aye, go ahead about your business before I choke your stupid ass."

"Oh, now you can talk, right? Just a minute ago your stank ass was acting like a mute. I was trying to be civil with you bastard, but you want to play games and I'm not that bitch to play with." The tears were falling uncontrollably now. How did we get to this point? Before all of this happened, we were planning a wedding, we were happy. He grabbed me by the throat and pushed me forcefully into the wall.

"You think everything is about you, but it's not. You go against everything a nigga tells your stupid ass because you think Dior is always right. You made a scene at the hospital for nothing. You had an attitude with a nigga for nothing. I'm really tired of that shit yo. I love you to death Dior, you are it for me, but you selfish as fuck ma. You were giving me your ass to kiss and for what? Because I was making sure my son's mother was straight." He pushed off of me and I hit my head against the mantle. I was pissed now. I charged at him and started swinging. He was letting me deliver blow after blow, until I started getting tired. Chance slapped the spirit out of my ass. I couldn't believe he hit me. I know I was just beating his ass, but still. I was crying my heart out and he just stood there, staring at me. The look in his eyes wasn't the look of pain or I'm sorry, but more so of you better not try that shit again. This is not the man I fell in love with, the father of my child, my best friend. How could he hurt me like this?

"I can't believe you put your hands on me Chance, how could you?"

"I'm sorry ma. You just don't get it and I hate that about you. Why the fuck you so insecure ma? A nigga never gave you a reason to feel like you not worthy of having all of me, that's just something within you that you need to work on. I should never have to put my hands on you, that ain't me, but no bitch is going to put her hands on me neither."

"That's what I am Chance, just some bitch? I went against my brother for you and that's how you feel?"

"Out of everything I just said, you only heard me say the word bitch? That's the shit I'm talking about."

I was pissed, but the hurt outweighed all of that. I was crying my eyes out, the pain cut deep. "Get out Chance. Get the fuck out, I hate you."

He walked towards me and tried to console me, "I'm sorry babe. I never meant for shit to be like this. Maybe we need some space to figure this shit out." He got up and walked towards the door. "I love you Dior. It's us…" I shook my head. I couldn't speak, the pain had my tongue stuck. He left out without looking back.

"Never them," I whispered. The words Chance spoke to me bruised my soul. I got myself together to go check on my baby. This situation with Chance will not get the best of me. I still have to tend to my kids first. I needed to get out of this house. This nigga put his hands on me and that is the ultimate no no. I needed my mother more than ever, but of course she wasn't there, she never was, so I called Jas to vent.

"Hey boo, what's up?"

"Hey," I said through tears.

"D, what's wrong? Why are you crying? Do I need to pull up bitch? Pregnant or not, a bitch on go."

"It's Chance. We got into it and his bitch ass put his hands on me."

"Oh hell nah, bitch I'm on the way." Leave it to Jas to turn up before I gave her the rundown on what happened. It didn't matter because my best friend was on the way, and right now, that's all I needed.

Chapter 6

Jas:

I have been staying to myself lately, trying to get used to being pregnant by an asshole. I sure wasn't expecting Dakota to be home so soon because of the massive charges that he had. I was almost five months pregnant and I couldn't wait for this to be over. My best friend called me and the sound of her voice really got me worried. The last time I heard her so down was when Chance was shot, so for him to be the reason of her pain, was a pain in itself. I finally built up the strength to get out of bed and get dressed. I put on a long Christian Dior maxi dress with a pair of Miu Miu sandals. I brushed down my wrap and applied a light touch of MAC lip gloss. I grabbed my Hilde Paladino bag and rushed out of the door. Dakota had been blowing my phone up all night, trying to come over and talk, but until my baby arrived, I felt there was nothing to talk about. My phone started ringing once again and I answered, frustrated by how he was working my nerves.

"What do you want?"

"Yo, lower your fucking voice. Where you at Jas? Don't make me pipe the fuck up, you know I will, bald head ass girl."

"I am on my way to your sister's house. Why the fuck are you bothering me? What do you need to talk about?"

"Aye, I need to holla at you, so you better hit my jack before this night is over or we will have a major problem."

"Yeah whatever, I might." With that said, I hung up. I was so over him and his games, especially when I didn't owe him nothing.

I wish I could believe you

Then I'll be alright

But now everything you told me

Really don't apply

To the way I feel inside

I rode through the city with Beyoncé's "Resentment" playing and I swear each lyric touched my soul. For two years, Dakota acted like he really cared about me, but the entire time, he was lying and had a whole female at home, playing house. I'll admit I'm still crushed and that alone makes me hate him even more. I got out of the car and went to knock on Dior's door, and to my surprise, Chance answered. He was leaving out as I entered.

"What up, Jas? She upstairs, I'm out."

I shook my head at him as I walked up the stairs, towards Dior's room. When I walked in, she was sitting in the middle of the bed, spaced out. I don't know what was going on, but my girl was down bad.

"Hey boo, where is Cayleigh?"

"She's in her room sleeping. Jas, I'm losing my mind."

I sat on the bed next to her so that I could console her. Just for this moment, I would put my problems to the side and be there for her.

"What's going on Dior? This is not like you."

"After all the shit I went through to get him back to me, he acts like I was in the wrong. We had a heated argument at the hospital because I wanted him to come home with me and our daughter, but he insisted on staying with Moe. All I asked was that he put himself in my shoes and ask where I was coming from." She started crying. "Ever since that day, we haven't said more than two words to each other. He comes home, spends a little time with the kids, then leaves without so much as a goodbye. I was fed up with him treating me that way, so I went downstairs to talk to him about it and shit went left. I don't know Jas, maybe I was wrong for coming off as a selfish bitch, but I just want things to go back to how they were when we were happy."

"D, you know I'm your best friend and I will always give it to you straight cut, no fold. When it came to you going to save him, that was not something you should have done. Now, don't get me wrong, I know you go hard for the people you love, but as a man, he feels weak because his bitch had to save his life. No man should ever have to question his manhood when he gets in a situation and his lady gets him out of it before he can show his strength. When it comes to the Moe situation, yes, you are being selfish. Think about it, Christian has had to deal with the fact that his mother died and had to adjust to being around a new woman every day of his life. Come to find out, his mother was very much alive, yet fighting for her life. Of course he is supposed to sit with her in case she pulls through and get information on why she left. You never know what's going through a nigga's mental, sis. You just need to ride it out and be patient with him."

I could tell that she was taking in everything I said. "Get dressed bitch. Let's go eat, we haven't blessed these streets together in a minute." Dior got dressed, and I had already got Cayleigh ready, so we hit the streets. I was going to help take my bestie's mind off of the bullshit, if only for the moment. We went to eat at Houston's. We both ordered the Hawaiian steak and potatoes, with lemonade. We chatted for what seemed like forever and I really enjoyed it.

"Excuse me ma, can I rap with you for a sec?" Jesus this nigga was fine. He had an angelic face, just my type. He was about 6'0, light skin, green eyes, but what turned me on the most was those pretty ass gold teeth. I slid out of the booth and he immediately looked at my growing belly.

"Hey, up here." He was so caught up in looking at my stomach, he forgot what he came for.

"Damn ma, I saw you walk in, but didn't see you had a youngin in there. What's up though, what's your name?"

"Jas, what about you?"

"I'm Carlos, but you can call me Los." He gave me his number and told me to call him when I was free. I damn sure was going to do so.

King:

I love Dior more than life itself. I need her more than my last breath, but my patience is running very thin with her and her ways. True enough, I should have considered her point of view, but fuck that, I'm a grown ass man and I don't need my bitch out busting guns and killing motherfuckers. That shit is not sexy at all to me. Niggas on the street going to think a nigga some soft ass nigga that needed his lady to handle his lightweight. For her to think I would leave the mother of my son high and dry, is lame as fuck. I'm a man and she is the mother of my son, so what image would that put in his head if he ever found out I turned my back on his mother. What I didn't mean to do was put my hands on her. I would never intentionally hurt her, but I was over Dior and her games. I've been kicking it with this little chick named Adore that I met about two weeks ago and she seemed cool as fuck.

"So, tell me a little about yourself ma. Where are you from?"

"Hmm, let's see, I'm 24 and a graduate in psychology. I'm single of course, no kids, and I have one sister that I am extremely close with. I'm from here, but I moved to Massachusetts to attend college. I'm actually here on business. I will be here for about a month or so. What about you?"

"I'm 23, I have two sisters, two children, and as you know, I do have a girl."

"So, who was that with you when we met?"

"That was a nobody, trust me on that. My girl wouldn't be caught dead looking as rough as that bitch, but enough about all that, I didn't come over here to talk about my relationship. It's your choice to continue to fuck with me ma, but I need you to understand I'm not leaving my girl for nobody." We sat in silence for about five minutes, but I couldn't lie to her. I'm not a fake nigga. There is no halfway with me, I keep it a buck regardless.

"Are you hungry boo?" One thing I noticed in this short period of time about her is that she made sure a nigga stayed fed. We have chilled maybe two times, but this was our first time holding a conversation about each other. She was cool though, something like a breath of fresh air that I needed, because Dior stressed a nigga out. Adore was different from what I was usually attracted to, but something about her caught my eye. A lame nigga would say she was fat, but lil mama was far from it. She was thick as fuck and her complexion was smooth and beautiful.

"It depends on what you feeding me." I gave her my panty dropper smile. That shit always makes bitches come up out of them thongs.

She hit me on the shoulder, "It depends on what you want to eat and I might make it happen."

"Oh yeah, straight like that?"

"I'm grown boo, I have no time to play. No need to put a nigga on a thirty-day test and all that other shit. The chemistry between us is strong, so why not act on it." With that being said, she straddled me and tried to kiss me, but I turned my head. No lips touch mine but Dior's two sets. I pushed her up and started taking off my clothes, as she did the same. Baby girl was stacked in all the right places, but those hips had me in a daze. She pulled a rubber out of the drawer and rolled it down my wood with her mouth. She slid down slowly and started riding the dick slowly. I was biting my lip because she felt good as a muhfucka.

"Fuck, bounce that ass ma." Lil mama was putting that snapper on me.

"Mmm, yess, this dick feels good. I feel it in my stomach." She picked up her pace and had a nigga's toes curling.

"Argh," I grunted. *Smack, smack.* I gripped hold of her ass. I started choking her while she was riding me.

"I'm cumming, oh my God." I stood up and she had her legs wrapped around my waist, then started bouncing up and down, fast then slow. I was ramming the pussy and she was taking every inch I delivered. Every thrust I went in, she came down harder. I threw her on the bed on all fours and rammed into her tunnel from behind.

"Feels good, don't it?"

"YESSS, it feels so good." She started throwing that ass back and baby girl was throwing that shit like she was in the league. She almost had a nigga about to tap out.

"Fuckk! Damn this pussy gone get me in trouble." I wasn't lying either. I knew this wouldn't be the last time I slide up in it. I was setting myself up for failure. She came and I followed behind her. I went to hop in the shower so I could head home. It was just my luck when I noticed the fucking condom broke.

Chapter 7

Cali:

"What time are you coming to get me?"

"I don't know Cali, stop fucking calling and asking me that same got damn question. You need to be worried about if your punk ass brother going to be over there, because I'm not for the disrespect today."

"Rue, just hurry the fuck up." I didn't have time for the bullshit at all. I'm Cali, Chance's younger sister. My brother has been overprotective of me and my sister Chasity our entire life, but that shit doesn't bother me because I am a grown ass woman. I couldn't help that I was such a bad bitch and could have anything I wanted. I am 5'5, cinnamon complexion, slim waist, average size thighs, a nice round onion booty, with eyes that changed colors. I have dreads that stop mid back, so yes, I was past a ten on the scale in my opinion. I haven't been on speaking terms with him ever since he embarrassed me in front of my boyfriend Rue. Rue and I have been together going on five years, and I have no plans of going anywhere anytime soon. I met Rue one day me and my sister went to the mall, and we have been inseparable ever since.

"Chas, can you bring your ass on? It's getting late and I don't want to hear Chance and mama's mouth. You know Chance will come looking for us." It was cold as hell outside and we skipped school to hang with some friends at Cumberland Mall. We came here twice a month, just to kick it.

"I'm coming sis. Will you just wait five more minutes? I'm trying to find me a new fit." My sister was a pro booster; she could literally steal the clothes off your back and not get caught. I was standing outside of H&M, when this little cutie walked up to me.

"Aye, what's ya name ma?" He was adorable and his teeth were more than perfect. He was about 5'9, light skin, with shoulder length dreads and pearly white teeth.

"Cali, and what's yours?"

"My name Nyrue ma, but you can just call me Rue. You beautiful as fuck, how old are you?"

"Fifteen, I'll be sixteen in April. How old are you?"

"I might get in trouble fucking with you, are you worth it, because I'm seventeen."

Chasity finally came out, but walked off when she noticed I was occupied.

"I have to go, my sister is waiting on me. Give me your phone and when you ready, hit my line." I gave him my number and the rest was history.

We have had plenty of ups and downs, from me fighting bitches to fighting his ass on numerous occasions because he thought I was something to play with. I loved the hell out of him though. He was my first everything and I honestly felt that I didn't need or want anything else. I have had two abortions that nobody knew about because I'm just not ready to become someone else's mother and I planned on keeping it that way. Rue has been trying to lock me down for about two years now, but until I get a ring and his last name, I'm not going for it. I will not be a baby mama and I know Chance would flip out. Chance is going to kill me anyway if he ever found out about the lifestyle I lived. You see, when I first met Rue, he had recently moved here from Miami. I heard he was the man there, but when he got here, it was hard for him to get on since he didn't know anybody, so he ended up starting his own record label. He still did his lil thing on the side, and that's where I always came in to play. Every other weekend, I would drive his work from here to Miami and give his product to his workers. I would collect the money before I came back. He didn't want me doing it, but I figured I would have a better chance of delivering than he would. Tonight, I had to take nine keys to Miami and drive back tomorrow night. I was packing my bag and noticed I couldn't find my new shoes I bought.

"Chas, have you seen my new Balenciaga sneakers I bought the other day? You better not have worn them."

Me and my sister were thick as thieves growing up, but the closer me and Rue grew, the further me and Chas drifted apart. I was convinced she was jealous of my relationship for some reason. Chas never believed in getting her own man, and preferred the sideline, over falling in love. I always told her she was too pretty to settle for less, but it always fell on deaf ears.

"Why would I wear your shoes, Cali? Don't try me like I can't afford my own."

"I just asked a question. A simple yes or no would have been just fine."

"Whatever Cali. No, I don't know where they are, maybe you left them in your little boyfriend's car."

"And here comes the shade. Ok Chas, you said no, so you can exit stage left." See what I mean? It's like she always finds a way to bring Rue into any situation. I was starting to believe she wanted my nigga, but it would be a cold day in hell before she even got close to him.

I couldn't wait until the summer so that I could move in with my man and start working towards a family. I was so over my sister and her attitude. I don't know what happened to us, but I would be damned if I kissed her ass to find out. I put on my Bebe romper with a pair of Bebe sandals and I was ready. Rue called and said he was outside, so I went to say goodbye to my mother before I left.

"Mom, I'm going to stay the weekend with Rue, I will see you Sunday night."

"Ok Cali, be safe. Strap it up and twerk on it," she started trying to twerk like always. My mother was a mess and a half, but I loved her though. Joyce was always somewhere trying to twerk, as if she could. I grabbed my bags and headed out, when I returned home, I would be fifty thousand dollars richer.

Cody:

I finally got Bree to give a nigga another chance and I planned on making the best of it. We done had more bad times than good, and I don't want my sons growing up thinking that it's ok to drag a female. I was headed over to see Jas and tell her I wanted to be strictly about my child and nothing else. Any other female I would have asked for a DNA test, but I know for a fact I was the only nigga digging in them guts; she was too in love with a nigga. Surprisingly, Bree hadn't said anything about Jas and her baby yet, but I knew the time was coming for us to have that discussion. She will have to accept my child and I want my sons to know their other sibling. I pulled up at Jas' house, ready to get this shit over with. I didn't know what the outcome of this would be. She told me the door was unlocked, so I just walked right in. Jas was sitting on the couch watching TV, and she was looking sexy as fuck. Her stomach had grown since the last time I saw her and she had such a beautiful glow. Fuck, this was about to be hard, but it has to be done.

"So what up ma, how you been?"

"Sick as hell, but I'm managing. What were you so anxious to see me about?" Damn, a nigga must be slipping because she was talking to me, but wouldn't even look my way.

"Damn ma, look at me while I'm talking to you." She turned off the TV, then turned facing me, sitting in Indian style.

"Yes, Dakota, what is it?"

"Alright ma, check this out." I was nervous as fuck. "I'm back with Bree and I want a clean slate, so whatever me and you had is done. I just want to strictly be about my seed. You don't have to worry about shit though. As long as you have my seed, I will put ten thousand dollars in your account every month." She looked at me as if she was disgusted, as her eyes became glossy.

"I don't need your money, Dakota. As a matter of fact, I don't need anything from you. I'm so over you and your childish ass games. You bring your tired ass over here to tell me you're done with me, but the funny thing is, I was done with you the day I got pregnant. Were you that stupid to think I would continue to play ping pong with another bitch over you, when you not doing a damn thing for me but dicking me down and throwing me money here and there." She stood up and started walking towards her door. "You said what you had to say, so are we done here?"

"Jas, I know I—"

She cut me off, "Save the bullshit Dakota. There will be no need for you to contact me until this baby comes. I'm so over this shit with you, GET OUT."

I shook my head as I walked out of the door, but stopped to say one last thing, "Don't ever think I played you, Jas. I do love you ma and that's real shit. I just fell in love with Bree and I'm sorry if I hurt you. I didn't do it intentionally."

"I'm sure you didn't." And with that, she closed the door in my face. I would be lying if I said that me hurting her didn't mean shit, because believe it or not, I felt bad as fuck. Jas has been around damn near my whole life, and seeing her hurt did something to me. I regret we even took that step, but what's done is done and we have a child to take care of when it's all said and done. I went over on Bellview Ave. to check on one of my spots and collect my cash. When I pulled up, I immediately got pissed. There were two bitches sitting on the porch, smoking what I was sure to be my product, and niggas hanging in the front, rolling dice and shit. I slammed my car door, pulled my pistol from my waist and shot in the air twice. They all jumped from the sound and looked at me with fear.

"So this what the fuck I'm paying y'all motherfuckers for, right? I'm paying y'all to chill with bitches and smoke up my shit when you supposed to be selling? Aye, get these bitches off my got damn property. If you don't work for me, you need to beat your fucking feet." I pay these niggas too much fucking money for them to be sitting on their ass, not watching shit around them.

"Aye boss, we were just taking a little break, business been a little slow—" This nigga Fred was on some dumb shit and I wasn't hearing it, so I cut his ass off.

"A break? I don't pay you niggas for breaks. Where the fuck is Keem and Lil Dave?"

"They went to the movies with some bitches." I couldn't believe this shit. I'm losing money and these niggas on double dates and shit. I was pissed the fuck off.

"So I guess you niggas in charge now, huh? Aye Dyno, let me holla at you."

"What up boss?"

"Explain to me why Fred saying business slow. Fred, go get my fucking money."

"I don't know what that nigga talking about boss. Business ain't changed, shit been moving."

Fred came back with two duffle bags and threw them in the trunk of my Panamera. I took my .45 from my waistline and gave Fred two to the dome.

"Call the crew and clean this shit up. Don't ever let me pull up and you niggas kicking shit like it's not money to be made." I hate I had to do Fred like that, but I didn't have time to be babysitting niggas. His excuse wasn't good enough. I didn't need excuses, I needed results.

Chapter 8

Dior:

Stressed would be an understatement to describe the way I felt. My relationship was damn near nonexistent and I'm not feeling this shit, not even a little bit. It had gotten to the point where he barely even came home, and he still doesn't say anything to me. I am literally losing my mind and I am horny as hell. It has been over a month since our relationship took a turn for the worst and a bitch was just about fed up. I needed to get out of this house and go have some fun before I do some shit I would later regret. I sent Chance a text to see if he was coming home so that he could watch Cayleigh for a while.

> **Me: Are you coming home? I wanted to go out for a while.**

> **Hubby: Where you going?**

Now I don't know if I was tripping or not, but I could not believe this nigga was questioning me like we been good and he had a right to. He didn't give me a chance to respond before he started calling.

"I see your phone still works, but whatever, are you coming home or not?"

"Where the fuck you think you going though? Don't play with me Dior, what you on?"

"Whoa now, hold up, don't try to check nothing nigga. I'm not on shit, I just want to go hang out with some friends and clear my head, so are you coming or nah?"

"You got a whole house to yourself. Do some yoga or some shit to clear your head, you don't need to go nowhere. I'm coming, but you not going nowhere." He hung up like he was really running shit. I couldn't believe he was trying to run shit like he was the king. I heard my baby girl on the monitor, so I went to her room to get her out of the crib. I heard the front door open and in walked the devil himself.

"So you going to tell me where you were going or what?"

"What do you mean were? I am going, why you acting like you care?" He walked up in my personal space and I gave him the evilest look I could give.

"Really Chance? It's that bad, huh?"

"What the fuck you talking about?"

"So you really going to bring your stupid ass up in here smelling like some stank, musty ass bitch, and think you about to touch my daughter. Nigga, you got me all the way fucked up." I laid Cayleigh in her bassinet and started swinging on him with all the strength in my body.

"Yo, keep your fucking hands off me, you remember what happened last time."

Tears poured from my eyes, I couldn't believe he has been cheating on me.

"How could you Chance? How could you do this to me?"

"Dior, you tripping ma, it's not even like that." He reached for my arm and I snatched it back.

"Don't you ever fucking touch me. You foul Chance, real foul." I thought we would get back to our happy place, but he went to another woman for comfort. The man I wanted to marry was cheating on me. I felt my chest closing in, it cut so deep. I went into the closet, snatching all of his clothes from it and throwing his shoes in the middle of the floor.

"Aye, what the fuck are you doing? You tripping ma. I ain't did shit, I swear."

"GET THE FUCK OUT AND DON'T YOU EVER FUCKING COME BACK." I snatched my ring off of my finger and threw it at him. I hated this man. I was disgusted with who I once loved. He grabbed me and I fell into his chest, pouring out my eyes.

"Listen to me ma, I'm sorry bae. I swear I didn't mean this shit. I'm man enough to admit my faults, but I'm not going nowhere. I know we been fucked up, but I don't want to be like this any longer. I need you Dior, a nigga been going crazy without you. I need you more than I need my next breath. Don't do this ma, we got plans. It's us, never them, remember?" I wanted to believe him, I swear I did, but right now I just couldn't. I know I could be a bitch sometimes, but he was supposed to be patient with me. I never thought Chance would do this to me, I was for sure he loved me.

"Chance, why? Why? Why?" I couldn't stop the pain, my heart was aching.

"I don't know bae, I wasn't thinking. I swear I'm sorry. We're going to get this shit right, we just have to take it slow."

He was saying all the right things with the wrong situation. Had he come home any other day and said sorry for what we were going through, I would have taken him back, no questions asked, but this situation was different. What pisses me off even more is he didn't even have enough respect for me to wash the bitch's scent off of him. Within this month, I have cried more over him than I have cried in my lifetime. I was all cried out. After Drake cheated on me repeatedly, I promised myself I would never allow another man to do this to me, and here I was, going through the same exact shit. This wasn't his first time doing this to me, so I was convinced it wouldn't be the last.

"I need some space."

"Space? What the fuck you need space for?" How could he be mad though?

"Just give me time to think about this, please."

"Yo Dior, I said sorry ma I—" I cut him off, I didn't want to hear the excuses.

"Chance, I can't do shit with a sorry, just give me some space please."

He stood up to leave, but what he didn't know was I was conflicting with myself whether I would allow him to come back. I guess this was my karma and what came with being the enemy's backbone.

Bree:

My sister being home has been such a breath of fresh air because it helped me not to stress over my complicated situation with Dakota. I decided to give him another chance, but I was proceeding the situation with caution, since he was so unpredictable. I was going on eight months and planning my baby shower. I didn't plan on doing anything too big, since I didn't really care for my family, nor did I have a lot of friends. My sister was helping out a lot, so I really didn't have to do too much. So far, Dakota has been doing pretty good when it came to this relationship and coming home at a decent time. There was one thing we needed to discuss though. We never talked about his situation with Jasmine and his baby that he was expecting with her. It had been weighing heavy on my mind, so I knew it was time to express my feelings about it.

"Babe, come here." He came out of the bathroom and sat at the foot of the bed.

"What's wrong ma?"

"We need to talk about your outside situation and what you plan on doing about it."

"Outside situation?"

"Come on Dakota, don't act slow. What's going on with you and Jasmine?" He dropped his head and let out a frustrated sigh."

"Well since we started over, I said I would keep shit a buck with you at all times. I went to see her the other night."

"Ok, and?"

"I just told her we were back together and that I couldn't fuck with her no more on that level and only wanted to be there for my baby. I know this situation makes shit harder to deal with, but I can't leave her to take care of my seed by herself, I'm not that type of nigga. Look Bree, I know it's going to take some time for you to trust me again, but I told you I got you and I meant that. I'm trying to do right by you and my sons." The funny thing about this was that I believed him. I was searching his eyes, trying to read his soul, and I felt he sincerely meant what he was saying.

"Dakota, I would never want you to abandon your child. I may be many things, but I am far from selfish. At the end of the day, that is an innocent child and it did not ask to be here. Now I know that there will be days when you want your baby to come spend time with you, so for the sake of the kids, I am willing to be cordial with Jasmine, but I need her to understand I can be that bitch that will tap that ass if she comes for me. I have spared her twice already, third strike she out." He started laughing, but I was more than serious. He stood up and kissed me on my forehead and I pushed him on the bed. I straddled him while taking off his shirt. My Cody knew he was sexy. I didn't have anything on from our previous session the night before. I unbuckled his pants and he told me to lay back. He took off his pants and started kissing on my body, careful not to miss any spots. When he came face to face with my kitty, he slowly entered his tongue into the honey jar and went to work.

"Ooh, yesss." He was tongue fucking the hell out of my kitty.

"Mmm, this pussy so sweet ma, shit." He started vibrating his tongue fast then slow, slow then fast. I started throwing my cat back on his tongue, squeezing his tongue with my kitty muscles. He started licking from my tunnel to my ass. He stuck his finger in and did a come here motion towards my g-spot and my legs started shaking.

"I'm about to cum, DON'T STOP!" I was screaming to the top of my lungs. I was moaning until I went hoarse. He slid in and started slow stroking, driving me insane. I tried running from the pleasure he was delivering, but he locked my legs with his arms.

He started whispering in my ear, "I love you ma, don't you ever forget. Fuck." He slowed down and I started squeezing his dick as I threw my cat back at him.

"I love you too daddy. It feels so good."

"Whose pussy is this?"

"All yours. Forever yours. I'm cumin again."

"That's right, cum on your dick."

He picked up his pace and I felt my body about to explode.

"Fuck, Bree, I'm about to bust."

I came all over his dick and the sheets and he followed behind, shooting his load inside of me, collapsing on top of me.

"Get your heavy ass up, you smashing my babies."

"Oh shit, I'm tripping." He rolled over and went to take a shower. I got up and took my linen off the bed to throw it in the washer. After that, I hopped on Facebook to see the latest news. It was always something on there about different thots at school. The shit was ridiculous. I kind of missed Clark Atlanta and couldn't wait to have my babies so I could go back. Dakota came out of the bathroom wrapped in nothing but a towel. I instantly got wet all over again, but Ms. Pearl had taken a beating two days in a row, and she was sore. It's one thing I couldn't deny when it came to him, and that was that he knew how to put it down, or maybe I was dick crazy. I got up and fixed Daddy something to eat. Cody, my Cody. I loved my nigga and fuck who didn't like it.

Chapter 9

King:

I fucked up, I fucked up bad. I felt like shit for hurting Dior like this. We've been fighting so much lately and a nigga just needed somebody in my corner, but it turned into more than that with Adore. I'm not saying I could ever leave Dior, because I would never do that, but being around Adore really calms my nerves. She didn't nag a nigga, she made sure I was fed, and she was a beast in the bedroom. It's been a month since me and Dior separated, and even though I was laid up with Adore, Dior was all I could think about. I was still able to see Cayleigh and Christian, but the thing that's fucked up is I was always getting my babies from Jasmine's crib. Yeah, it was that bad. She didn't even want to see a nigga's face. My phone started ringing and took me away from my thoughts.

"Yooooo."

"Hello, this is Dr. Gray from Grady Memorial Hospital. I am looking for Mr. Chance McCray."

"This is he."

"I was calling to inform you that Monique has awaken from her coma and asked for you. I see that you left your number as a next of kin." Damn, I been so tied up with my bullshit I haven't been to see Moe.

"I'm on the way and thank you," I hung up and jumped up to get dressed. I threw on my Nike jogging suit with a pair of white Forces and ran down the steps.

"Where you going? I was just cooking dinner."

"I'll be back ma, wrap that shit up."

I wasn't in the mood for all of her questions, especially when she not my lady, nor will she ever be. I hopped in my candy apple red Jeep SR/T and peeled out. It took me about twenty minutes to get to Grady, due to the afternoon traffic. I got a text notification from Adore.

Adore: That's fucked up. I slaved over this hot ass stove, just for you to leave without eating.

Me: Something important came up.

I don't know where all this was coming from. She hasn't been tripping, so I would like for her to keep it that way. No side bitch will try to check me about anything. I missed the hell out of Dior, and when I left the hospital, I planned on taking my ass home. She has had more than enough space. I walked into Moe's room and she was laid back, looking at *Maury*. She looked my way and shook her head. "Chance, let me explain..." Call me selfish, but I wasn't trying to hear that shit.

"Explain what Moe? If you not explaining how the fuck you knew Marco, I don't want to hear shit."

"I only remember bits and pieces of everything, but I will try my best to explain this to you." She started telling me what she remembered from meeting him, up until when he shot her. She didn't know anything about him being my brother and wanting to kill me, at least that's what she said. She told me how he would beat her ass every day for no reason at all. I could tell there were more pieces to the puzzle, but if she couldn't remember, I would just have to take that shit as lost information.

"You really hurt me Chance. You turned your back on me when you said you never would, all because I wouldn't set somebody up."

"But the next nigga asked you to do the same thing and you jumped at the opportunity. Fuck out of here, ain't no excuse for that shit ma." She started crying, but she could cry me a river because she was fucked up for this.

"I knew you wouldn't understand. Nobody was intentionally supposed to get hurt and I definitely wasn't supposed to be in a damn coma." She started shaking her head, "I want to see Christian, I miss him so much."

"I don't think that's a good idea right now. This shit is too much and we have to take all this shit slow. He is only four years old and thought you were dead, so to pop up still alive would confuse him. Give me some time to tell him what's going on."

"You telling me I can't see my own son? Why Chance, huh? You got your little bitch playing mommy?"

"You still the same selfish, jealous ass person you were before. You sitting in a damn hospital, just got through fighting for your life, and your main concern is what the next bitch is doing to your son. I didn't come here for this Moe."

I know she was hurt, but fuck that. I don't fully trust what she told me and I refuse to let her hurt my son again.

"I guess I can do that. I really didn't want him to see me here anyway. We can wait until I am completely healed and out of here. Thank you Chance. My nurse told me you were here majority of the time, but you stopped coming. Why did you stop?" Damn, I didn't expect for her to ask no shit like this, but fuck it. She was a tad bit bipolar or something because she was thanking me after she went off not even two minutes ago.

"Dior felt like I was choosing you over her because I was spending all of my free time with you."

She turned her nose up and let out a frustrated sigh. "That bitch really has one hell of a hold on you. You really need to wake the fuck up Chance. Just let me see my son." She folded her arms across her chest and started looking out the window.

"I'll be back to check up on you later. Don't be mad at me Moe, I got you." She didn't say shit and I didn't have time to beg her ass to understand. Hell, I didn't even understand why I stopped coming, I just know I did it. I left the hospital and headed home to my family.

Cali:

I came back to the city fifty thousand dollars richer and I must say, I was feeling quite lovely. I wanted to go to Saks

Fifth to do some major shopping and blow a couple of stacks on myself. I went to my mom's house to see if Chasity wanted to ride with me so I could buy her some things. Even though she pissed me off before I left, I still loved my sister regardless. She was in the shower when I walked in, "Chas, you want to ride with me to the mall to get a couple of things, or you have something to do?"

"Yeah, I'll ride, give me a second to get dressed." I always made sure my little sister was straight. She ate when I ate, even though she had her own money. I went to sit on the porch and waited for Chas, since my mom wasn't here, and sparked me up a blunt. I was sitting, staring at my car and I decided it was time to upgrade my lil baby. I had a 2013 Lexus Coupe, but I needed something that screamed "Boss Bitch" when I'm riding down the street. After we left the mall, I will be going to a car dealership.

"Ok sissy, I'm ready to go."

My sister was bad, hands down, but sometimes her attitude could take away from it. Chasity was 5'3, bright skinned, and kept her hair fire red. Out of me, her, and Chance, I was the only one with pretty eyes, but you would think Chas had them too, because she always wore contacts. We had the same little onion booty, but Chas was a little bit thicker than me. We hopped in the car and headed to do a major shopping spree.

Dirty soda in a Styrofoam

Spend a day to get my mind blown

Dress it up and go to NASA

200 Miles on the dash

Got to roll a pound up and gas it

Switching lanes in a Grand Rapid

Future's "March Madness" always made me turn up, no matter what atmosphere I was in. I was high as hell, vibing to the music, and so was Chas.

"Bitch, let's go out tonight. Rich Homie Quan will be at the Compound tonight."

"Shit, I'm with it."

There were days me and Chas were thick as thieves, and there were days I hated her, but it was all love in the end. We went to Saks Fifth and Lenox and spent damn near fifteen thousand dollars a piece shopping. We didn't need anything for a while, with all the shit we got. I was tired from going back and forth, putting bags in the car because I couldn't carry it all. The trunk and back seat were full. It was seven o'clock when we were done and I worked up an appetite, so we went to the Cheesecake Factory to eat.

"So, where did Mommy go this time?"

"Girl, believe it or not, she went on a date. She met some dude honey and they went out on the town I guess. Joyce trying to get her groove back." I almost died laughing. I couldn't believe my mama's old ass was out with some dude. "Have you talked to Chance? I guess he's still mad at me from that day he came over."

"Yeah, he calls me damn near every day, you should call him."

"Nah, he needs to call and apologize to me, I didn't do shit wrong."

"I guess. It's been a while since we hung out, you be so busy and all."

"Come on Chas, don't start." Our food came out and we ate. I had the shrimp alfredo and Chas had the chicken alfredo. We left the restaurant and headed home to get dressed. I was so happy I got my locs touched up while I was in Miami because I didn't feel like dealing with my hair. I got in the shower and washed with my Love Spell body wash. I let the hot water hit my body before I stepped out. I was hoping Chasity's slow ass was getting dressed. I put on a black cat suit that hugged my body like a glove and made my ass sit up perfectly. My Agent Provocateur heels and choker made my outfit stand out more. I filled in my brows and applied MAC gloss to fill out my lips. I grabbed my Hermes clutch bag and headed to Chasity's room. "You about ready chick?"

"Yeah, let's roll." Chasity looked flawless in her BCBG body con dress that stopped mid-thigh. Her thigh high heels complemented the dress in every way. She flat ironed her hair bone straight and it stopped at her ass.

"Yesss, bitch yessss. My bitch bad, looking like a bag of money." I started bouncing my ass cheeks one by one.

"Bitch, you legit slow. Let's go." She grabbed her Lana Marks bag and we left. We pulled up to the Compound and the line was extra thick. I pulled around front and gave my keys to valet.

"Be careful with my baby and don't be joy riding in my shit." We walked to the front of the line to talk to the bouncer. All eyes were on us and you could hear bitches throwing hell of shade.

"Say, how much we have to pay to skip this line?"

"Eighty a piece." I gave him three fifty because we were not really old enough to be in here. The inside of the club was damn near packed to capacity. We got some drinks and it was time to turn up. Waka Flocka's song "No Hands" came on and we ran to the dance floor. I started making my ass clap. I was already high from smoking on the way here, so I was turned up. Chas had a scowl on her face and rolled her eyes, then I felt the hairs stand up on the back of my neck and knew the feeling all too well.

"Yo Cali, what the fuck you doing in here? You ain't say shit about no club and what the fuck do you have on?

"And neither did you say shit, so what's up? You want to turn up because you know I'm with the shits just as much as you are." He grabbed me by the arm and I snatched it away. "Rue, you better get your shit together, don't make me make a scene."

"Yo, come holla at me outside. Chasity, she will be back."

I turned to face Chas and she was giving Rue this seductive look. Tonight will be the night she tells me what the fuck her issue is with my man. We walked outside and he immediately started the bullshit. "Nyrue, since when do I have to check in with you about where I go? You not my damn daddy, boy I'm grown over here."

"When you decide to wear bullshit like that," he pointed at my outfit. "I should beat your ass for that shit. Go get Chasity and take your ass home." This nigga was on some more shit, but I was about to go back in and have me some fun. Fuck Nyrue and his feelings.

Chapter 10

Jas:

Dakota had me fucked up, pulling up on me with his bullshit. I wasn't tripping off of him at all, believe it or not, because since I met Los, we have been kicking it very heavy on a regular. He was thirty-two and held serious grown man status. I could never compare him to Dakota because unlike my baby daddy, he knew how a woman was supposed to be treated. When he comes over, he rubs my feet, gives me a back massage, and runs my bath water. Due to the fact that I'm pregnant, he hasn't gotten the cat yet, but baby, as soon as my pudding heals, he will be getting the business. He is sexy, smart, and caked up. He owns a car lot, an apartment complex, and he has a club down in Miami. He's been legit for about five years now and I am so happy that he's not in those streets. I feel like I did a major upgrade. I still had my guard up though because you can never be too sure with these niggas. I had a doctor's appointment today to find out what I was having and I was so excited. Los wanted to go with me, but I didn't think that would be appropriate. Besides, Dakota had asked to go first.

Me: Were you still going to the doctor with me or nah?

Baby daddy: Yeah, it's at 3, right?

Me: Yes. See you there.

Baby daddy: (smiley face emoji)

I put on my pink and gray PINK outfit and my shiny pink Uggs. I put my hair up in a messy bun and was ready to go. I Facetimed Los to let him know I was headed to the doctor and to see if he wanted to go out to eat afterwards.

"What's up baby girl, everything good?"

"Hey babe. Yeah, everything is copacetic, except for the fact I kind of miss your big head ass."

"Oh yeah? What you got going on? I'm at the lot right now, slide through. Let me see that sexy face up close and personal."

"Well, I have to go to the doctor, remember? I'm headed there now, but I was calling to see if you wanted to go eat afterwards."

"I think I can do that. Ol' boy still going with you?"

"Yeah, that's what he says." One thing about us, we kept it all the way one hundred with one another.

"Ok cool, hit my jack when you get done and don't be giving my kisses away."

"Boy bye, ain't no kisses bih." We both started laughing and hung up. I really liked Los, but I still had a piece of me that was scared he would come with drama. I knew he had two children, but they lived in Chicago and came here during summer breaks, so baby mama drama I knew I wouldn't have to deal with. I pulled up to the doctor's office and found a parking space. I signed in and took a seat, until my name was called. I scrolled social media to pass time by and a text came through.

Bestie: Cody told me about your appointment, make sure you call me when you leave. I'm soooo excited.

Me: I will call you when I'm done (kisses)

"Jasmine Walker?"

I stood up to walk towards the back and Dakota walked in. I just knew he wasn't going to show up, but I guess he proved me wrong.

"What up ma? Traffic was a little fucked up, but I made it." He smiled that smile that I once loved.

"Hello, Mommy and Daddy. Today is a special day, isn't it? Are we excited?"

"Yes." I wasn't lying, I couldn't wait to see what my little munchkin was.

She put the cold gel on my stomach and I immediately got hype.

"Well, it looks like we have a healthy baby girl."

I was ecstatic I was having a little diva. Dakota was smiling from ear to ear. Now he had his two princes and a little princess. He stood up and kissed my stomach and gave me a lustful stare. Had our situation been different, I would have cherished this moment, but I just wasn't trying to be in that space anymore.

"Thanks for coming Dakota. It really meant a lot that you made it."

"Ain't nothing Jas, I told you I got you. On the real though, you know she will have two big brothers and I want my kids to grow up together, so what you think about having a conversation with Bree? I don't want it to be any bad blood between the two of you because it will affect the kids in the long run."

"I have no problem with that. I'm not on that anymore. I just want to do right by my baby girl."

"Aight, bet. I'm going to set something up."

We left out of the office and parted ways. I was ready to see my lil boo.

Me: IT'S A GIRL!!!

Bestie: Yessss bitch. So, it's time to do some shopping. I'm cooking dinner Sunday and I want you to come and bring your boo.

Me: Ok, we can do that. Talk to you later.

I called Los to see if Los was ready to go eat dinner or not.

"Yoooo."

"That is not how you answer the phone, get it together. What are you doing?"

"Shit, a little paperwork, where you at?"

"I'm on my way to you, are you ready?"

"Yeah, push up on me." He was so hood and it turned me on in the worse way.

"Alright babe, I'll be there in twenty. The sun was beaming so I threw on my Chanel frames and let my top down. I pulled in to Los' car lot and he was standing outside, talking to some female. By the looks of things, they were having a heated argument. I would be sure to ask who she was. Los and the young woman started walking towards my car.

"Baby girl, this is Bailey; Bailey, this is my girl Jas."

We never established that we were an item, so I was shocked by his introduction.

"Hey Jas, nice to meet you. She is pretty bro. I'll hit you up later and let you know what she says."

"Yeah, do that ma." She walked off and he looked at me, smiling, then grabbed me into a hug.

"No need to be thinking all hard and shit, ma. That's my baby mama's little sister, she wants me to get custody of my kids."

"Is something wrong with them?"

"Nah, not really. She just said her sister was struggling with them. I don't see how because I send more than enough money every other week."

Something wasn't right about his baby mother and I wasn't going to stress what it was.

Dior:

Since Chance and I split last month, I have been doing a lot of soul searching. I have pretty much come to terms that my relationship was over and I am learning to be just fine with it. Chance hurt my soul when he cheated on me. I was stressed to the point that I was losing weight. Then he had the audacity to put his hands on me and that broke me down even more. We haven't seen each other because our drop off and pick up place was Jas' house. I missed him so much though and I couldn't deny that. I planned to have everyone over for dinner tomorrow because it gets lonely being that it was just me and the kids. My doorbell rang and I had no idea who would be coming by unannounced. I put on my robe and headed to the door. It was Chance and my first thought was *why he didn't use his key,* then I remembered that I had changed the locks.

"What are you doing here? Cayleigh is with the nanny and Christian is at school."

"I'm aware of that. I came over so that we could talk please."

I would be lying if I said he didn't look good as hell. He had on a black and red Armani Exchange fit with a pair of black and red number 11 Jordan's. I could tell he just came from the barbershop because his cut was neat and fresh, not that he didn't keep it that way. I stepped aside and motioned for him to come in.

"So, what do you want to talk about?" I asked without making eye contact. I knew I was still weak for this man and there was no denying it.

"First off Dior, I want to apologize for everything I ever put you through. Ma, you have to know I would never intentionally hurt you. I love you more than life itself. I want to come home with my family and I'm determined to make this shit right. I need you bae, I know you need me too."

"Chance, you want me, you don't need me. If you needed me, you wouldn't have hurt me this way. I'm just tired of the drama. I just want to be happy like we used to be."

"And I plan on getting us there, just let me come back home. I feel so incomplete ma. Without you and my kids, I'm nothing. Please give us another chance. I'm not a begging ass nigga, but I'm sitting here begging you. If you want to take shit slow, I'm cool with that, as long as I'm here with you. I miss you. I miss your smile, I miss that morning breath, I miss kissing you on your forehead when you feel down, but most of all, I miss that sweet pussy. I know you miss Daddy and I know you miss me making love to you every night."

I smiled at his last comment because Lord knows I did miss it.

"How do I know you won't hurt me again?"

"You don't know, but what I want you to know that when I hurt you, I hurt myself."

He grabbed my hands and kissed the back of them. I had tears in my eyes because I had so many mixed emotions. A part of me wanted him to stop, but my heart yearned for him. He untied my robe and it fell to the floor. He stepped back and smiled, then bit his bottom lip. He picked me up bridal style, then carried me up the stairs, while kissing me oh so passionately. He threw me on the bed that we once shared and started to undress.

"You missed this pussy, daddy?"

"Hell yeah!"

"Come show me how much."

He pulled me to the edge of the bed and went into feast mode on my kitty. He was sucking as if he was searching for my soul.

"Mmm, yess."

"That feel good ma, don't it?"

"Ooh yesss, I'm about to cum." I did just that and he slurped up every ounce of juices I released. He started tongue fucking me and massaged my ass cheeks gently. He stuck his finger in my pot and started the come here motion, attacking my g-spot. I started trying to run, but he locked my legs with his arms.

"Oh God, I can't take it."

He stood up, slid in and started slow stroking with a slow rhythm. This man was making love to my body like never before. His dick game was screaming he was sorry. I started grinding upwards, meeting each thrusts.

"Fuckk, ma, this pussy feels good. I missed this shit so much."

I had my hands on his waist, guiding him in and out of my cat, while watching him thrust in and out of my opening. He squatted over me, pushed my legs behind my head and dropped the head in and out slowly, while kissing all over my body.

"I'm cumin babe, ahh." I watched my kitty push what had to be six ounces of juices out and cream all over his dick.

"That's right, nut all over this dick and let him know you missed him."

He picked up his speed, hitting every wall my pussy contained. I felt it jerking, letting me know he released all of his seeds inside of me.

He fell on the bed next to me and laid there and I jumped up. I took every inch of his eleven inches in my mouth and I could taste my juices all over him. I took him down my throat and started humming sweet melodies on it. Squeezing his dick with my throat, I massaged each ball with my hands, showing them an equal amount of attention.

"What the fuck ma?"

I looked back and his toes were curled up, doing the Crip walk. I straddled him and started bouncing my ass up and down, taking turns making each ass cheek jump.

"This pussy treating Daddy good? Mmm, I'm about to cum again." His eyes were rolling every direction like he was cross eyed. I hit a split on the dick, then started riding him sideways.

"Shit, I'm..." I felt him release more kids inside of me. I went to get a rag to wipe us down and when I came back in the room, he was fast asleep. Like always, I made him tap out.

Chapter 11

Adore:

I have been trying my best not to catch feelings for Chance, but the more I tried, the harder they got. I have always been the type to keep my feelings under wraps, but with him, it had proven to be a little more challenging. I have been sick and throwing up my insides for the past week and I didn't know what it could be. I made a doctor's appointment, but that wasn't until next week, so I went to CVS and bought four different tests. It was just my luck they all came back positive. I was in conflict with myself on whether I should keep it or get an abortion. We always used protection, so how this happened, I had the slightest clue. I was also debating on whether I should even tell him. He has been a little distant lately and avoiding my phone calls, so I really was lost on what to do. My phone started ringing, bringing me out of my thoughts.

"Hello?"

"Well, hey stranger. You get you a new boo and forget all about your sis, huh?"

"Not at all, I just haven't been feeling my best. Is everything ok?"

"Of course, are you busy? I want to see you."

"No, pull up bitch."

"Ok, I'm on the way."

I had to get myself together because I knew I looked like shit. I didn't feel like myself and I refused to be one of those hoes that start looking dead once they got pregnant. I hopped in the shower and washed my body with Pure Seduction body wash. Once I got out, I rubbed myself down with French Vanilla body oil and put on my red lace thong set. It was nice out, so I put on a pair of Nike shorts with the matching top. I planned on enjoying my nice shape before this pregnancy got real...if I decided to keep it. I wet my hair in the shower, so I put a little mousse in it and wore it curly. For my shoes, I threw on a pair of Air Max 95s and I was ready if Bree wanted to hit the streets. I knew she would most likely want to go somewhere and walk, so I was more than dressed for the occasion. There was a knock on the door and I knew it was Bree.

"Hey boo, my nephews getting out there I see. What's up?"

"Don't remind me. They need to hurry up and come."

"Not before the baby shower I hope."

"To be honest sis, I don't even want one." I looked at her like she was out of her damn mind. If she knew like I knew, she better have one.

"You sound crazy, but I guess. So what's new? How are you and baby daddy?"

"So far so good, but you know how that shit goes. So, I really came over to ask did you want to go over to his sister's house for dinner tomorrow? She having a little get together and most likely Dakota's ratchet ass baby mama will be there."

"Wait, what? Bitch, what baby mama and why would that hoe be there? Bih, you ain't told me nothing about this. Who is she?"

"Honey, her name Jasmine and she's about three months behind me. She is his sister's best friend, so I know for a fact she will be in the building."

"Oh, y'all got some Jerry Springer shit going on. I guess I'll go. That bitch better not try to pop off because you know how I am."

"I doubt it. I already clapped on her and we supposed to be having a talk about these kids. Dakota already set her straight. So what's new with you?" I refused to tell my sister about me being pregnant because I had yet to go to the doctor to get confirmation. I guess I was just in denial.

"Shit, dealing with these crazy ass people. I have that session I was telling you about Tuesday, and honey, I'm really on edge about it. Her profile seems a bit much."

"Pray about it sis." Her phone started ringing and she told me wait a second, so I took that time to text Chance.

Me: So that's how we kicking it?

Chance: Man what's up?

Me: Don't do all that. I need to holla at you about something important. When are you free?

Chance: I'll get at you when I get time. I WILL CALL YOU.

Me: You on some other shit, but yeah, you do that.

I've never been a bitch that chased a nigga, and I would be damned if I start. I'm bad enough to get any nigga I wanted, so he really had me fucked up. I was going to talk to him about it, but I had made my mind up, I was not keeping this baby.

Cali:

Chasity was really pissing me off the way she always tried to handle Rue. I played a lot of games, but when it came to Nyrue Boykin, shit could get deadly really quick. So much was going through my mind as I sat at the car dealership, waiting for the keys to my new car.

"Thank you ma'am, enjoy your new ride.

"Indeed I will."

I was now the owner of a 2015 Range Rover. I had initially planned on trading in my Lexus, but hell, I got good cash, so I just bought me a Range. I called Rue to see where he was so that I could push up on him and let him see my new car.

"Baby, where you at?"

"I'm at the stu, what's up baby girl?"

"I have a surprise for you, I'm on the way."

"Bet."

I was beyond excited and a bitch was ready to flaunt all through the city. Migos "Pipe it Up" graced my speakers and I was dabbing while riding towards bae's studio. I pulled up to the studio and texted to let him know I was outside.

"Damnnnn bae, you doing big shit like that? Yo, this bitch is lit."

I stepped out of the car and jumped into his arms. He was looking so fucking sexy and I was horny as hell.

"I'm happy you like it papa. So how about some celebration sex."

"Shitt, run that shit baby, stop talking."

I was happy that nobody was at the studio because we were about to make some music of our own. We went into the recording room and I went into the booth. Rue cut the sound system and microphone on. Whenever we had sex at the studio, he would record our sounds and we would listen to our music sometimes at night, during pillow talk, and laugh about it. Yeah, I know we were weird as fuck, but I enjoyed the simple things. I slid my panties off as he made his way over to me. I had on a short maxi dress, so that was easy access. Rue started sucking on my neck roughly, as he stuck a finger inside my honey pot and started stirring it around. I let out a slight moan as he picked up the pace of his finger.

"Mmm, bae." I felt my juices running down my leg. I unbuckled his pants and as they fell, I started massaging his dick through his boxers and he became erect immediately. I pulled his boxers down and he lifted me up. I wrapped my legs around his waist and started bouncing up and down, while holding on around his neck.

"Ooh wee Cal, you wet as fuck." He was squatting and giving me the dick, sending my body into overdrive.

"Pearl is about to cum, go deeper."

"Cum for Papa then. I want all you got."

He put me down and I spread my legs wide, while holding on to the wall.

"Am I in trouble officer?" I handed him the handcuffs and he cuffed me.

"Hell yeah, spread them wider." I arched my back as he slid in swiftly. He started off slowly, then picked up his pace, drilling my insides.

"Ah, I can't...take...it."

"Take this dick like a big girl."

I started squirting everywhere and he continuously went deeper and deeper.

"This dick taking care of you?"

"Yessss, always."

"Cum with me then."

I did as I was told and I fell to the floor. He started laughing at me like the shit was funny.

"Let me find out this dick got you limping."

"Ha ha real funny." I forced myself to stand up and put my panties back on. His phone rang, so he stepped out to take the call. I grabbed our CD we just made and went to the bathroom.

"Bae, I got some work I need to go drop off right quick in Perry Homes, you want to run me over there? It's just a pound of gas, nothing major."

"Yeah, I'm not doing nothing, let's go." He put the bag in the trunk and hopped in the passenger seat. I turned the music up and Future's "Slick Talk" came through.

"Bae, yo nigga gave you taste I see."

"Boo please, I gave you flava, know that." We rode to the music and were having a good time, until I looked in my rearview and saw blue lights. Rue looked at me and followed my eyes, until he saw what I was looking at.

"Baby, what the fuck?"

"Chill Cal, everything going to be alright."

Two officers approached my car on each side, and to say I was scared would be an understatement.

"Is there a problem officer?"

"Yes ma'am, you were speeding, were you not paying attention?" The officer on Rue's side was looking through the windows, as if he was looking for something.

"Sir, step out of the car," the officer said. The devil is a lie if they think for one second they are about to search my car and lock him up. My officer went back to his car, as the other officer searched my truck. I have never been pulled over and the pigs would wait until today to do a search.

"Ma'am, you mind telling me what this is?"

My soul flew out of my body as he held up the duffel bag with the work in it.

"Who does this belong to?"

Rue stepped up and I stepped around him.

"It's mine sir." Rue shot me a look that would kill me, if looks killed.

"Cali, what the fuck you doing?"

"Shut up Rue, you don't have to lie for me. It's mine officer, he was just riding with me to make sure nothing happened to me."

I knew he was pissed, but he already had pending charges and I refused to lose him to the system. I have never been in trouble, so I knew I would be okay. The officer handcuffed me and for the first time, I was on my way to jail. All I could think about was the fact that Chance was going to kill me.

Chapter 12

Bree:

I was amazed at how much Dakota had changed. We were still a work in progress, but he had improved drastically. I woke up to breakfast in bed every morning, foot rubs, the whole nine. He made sure all my needs were met before he participated in the street life. I guess it was safe to say I was almost able to trust him again. Rashad had been blowing my phone up non-stop for the past two weeks, and I wish he would just let it go. He was acting like the real stalker type and he never even touched the cat. I told him I would meet up with him tomorrow, but I was only going to let his ass know to leave me the fuck alone because I was no longer interested. Dior's dinner was later on tonight and I wasn't the least bit excited to go. I talked Dakota into going with me, seeing that it was his people, but it wasn't easy since we heard her and Chance were back together. Adore was riding over there with us, so we had to stop by and pick her up later. I went downstairs to see what Dakota was doing and of course, he was playing the game and talking on the phone. I sat beside him on the couch and grabbed a controller.

"I want to play, so start the game over."

"Come on ma, I'm winning and shit. You trying to come fuck up a nigga mode. Say Black, let me hit your jack right back."

"You just scared to get your ass whipped, that's all, stop making excuses." I stood up and restarted the game. He was pouting like the big baby he was, but I wasn't moved by it at all.

"Oh, you really about to get your ass kicked now, cutting my shit off like you run shit. What we betting?"

"Boy bye, I'm not betting your cheating ass shit. You know damn well you be on some sneaky shit when you play people, so fall back."

We played the game for what seemed like forever. I had become tired, so I decided to take a nap before we headed out.

"I'm about to lay down for a while, are you coming?"

"Nah, I was going to go get a line-up and go check on a couple of spots. I'll be back before five though, and your fat ass better be ready."

"Now you know you trifling for calling me fat. Ain't nothing fat but this cat nigga, don't front."

"Oh yeah, wash that thang too because she smelling a lil tart." He started fanning his nose like he really smelled something.

"Not this squeaky clean pussy, you a damn lie. The way you slurp on it, I can't tell," I said, while throwing the pillow at him. I went upstairs to lay down for a few. I was sleep for about an hour, before my phone started ringing and woke me up out of my sleep. I answered without looking at the ID.

"Yeah!"

"Ugh bitch, you sound like a man."

"What do you want Adore, I was sleep?"

"What time y'all coming to get me? You said it started at 6:30, and bitch it's almost six o'clock, so what's up, we still going or nah? A bitch is hungry and I need to know if I need to go get me something."

"Yes hoe, we still going. Let me get my ass up. Why didn't you invite your boo, I'm pretty sure it wouldn't have been a problem."

"Girl, fuck him. I haven't even spoken to his ass, but anyway, toodles, and hurry your big ass up."

I called Dakota to see where he was and he said he was on the way. I jumped in the shower to wake myself up a little. Luckily, I had picked my clothes out earlier, so I threw on a Christian Dior jumpsuit and a pair of Red Bottoms. The jumpsuit was hugging my protruding belly and I looked like I was about to pop. I put my hair up in a messy bun and applied a light amount of nude MAC lip gloss. Dakota came running up the stairs.

"Damn baby, we might not make it to the dinner, you looking sexy as a muhfucka." He slapped me on the ass. "Aye, but that shit ain't suffocating my got damn babies is it?"

"Boy, let's go."

He helped me down the stairs and out to the car. We pulled off, in route to get Adore. Today was about to be an interesting day. We pulled to the hotel and Adore was standing outside, scrolling through her phone. Dakota honked the horn and I yelled out the window, "Come on bih."

"Hey Cody."

"What's going on Adore?"

My sister and Dakota met one time and I could tell she didn't too much care for him, but that was her problem, not mine. It took us about thirty minutes to get to Dior's house because traffic was a little jacked. As we were getting out of the car, I saw Jas and some guy walking up the driveway. He was one fine piece of work and had that thug appeal. Dakota's face went from a smile to a mean scowl. I could tell he was pissed, but I didn't understand why.

"So Jasmine, who is your little friend?"

"First off, he is not my little friend, he is a grown ass man. Second, his name is Carlos, if you must know." I just shook my head and wobbled around them because I wanted no parts of it.

"Come on Adore. Dakota, let's go now." We walked inside and Dior was setting up the table.

"Hey everybody, I will be done in one minute." Dakota went and picked up Cayleigh and the cutest little boy came running down the stairs.

"Christian, go wash your hands and tell your daddy it's time to eat."

"Yes ma'am."

I had never seen him before, but I assumed he was Chance's son. I guess she saw the confusion written on my face.

"Oh, that's Christian, Chance's son." She looked at Adore and extended her hand, "I'm Dior, and you are?" she asked my sister as she washed her hands.

"Oh I'm Adore, Bree's sister."

"Nice to meet you. Make yourself at home, I will be ready in one minute."

Chance came down the stairs and when he looked our way, he looked as if the wind was knocked out of his body. "What the fuck? What are you doing here?", he asked Adore. How the hell did they know each other? Here goes the bullshit.

Cody:

Being in the same house as this snake ass nigga wasn't what I had planned for my Sunday evening, but Bree insisted a nigga came over here. To top that shit off, Jasmine tried me, bringing this nigga up in my sister's house like he belonged or some shit. She moved on too got damn fast and I wasn't with that shit. Next thing you know, she going to be having my baby around this nigga, and that's when shit going to get ugly. I don't know why her bringing his ass here pissed me off, but it did. I carried my niece in to the dining room, where everybody else was, and locked eyes with Chance's bitch ass.

"Aye, you can stop looking at a nigga like that though, or you can get the fuck out."

"Nigga, this my sister's house, so if anybody is going to get out, it will be your lame ass. I don't even know why you here anyway."

"What's up nigga, you want to let some heat off? I've been waiting to tag your ass anyways from all the shit you were talking last time," he was taking his jewelry off. I laid my niece in her swing and walked up in his personal space.

"You ain't said shit but a word," I walked up and pushed him with so much force, he flew back a little. Now King had me by at least three inches, but a fuck I did not give, because I rolled with the best of them. He pushed me back, but I didn't budge, so I came through with a mean left uppercut and he followed suit. We went blow for blow and the ladies were yelling for us to stop. Jasmine's little boy toy grabbed me and Dior grabbed for Chance and he pushed her back. I broke free and hit him with a right hook and we went at it again. Dior punched both of us in the rib and that shit made me double over in pain.

"Yo Dior, what the fuck you do that for?"

"Y'all overgrown asses look real fucking childish. Do y'all not see these kids here? Sit the fuck down and let's eat. Ain't nobody got time for y'all to be fighting like some big ass kids."

"I got something for you my nigga," he said as he went to the bathroom to clean up. I'm not going to lie, that nigga gave me a run for my money. We both had a busted lip, but mine wasn't leaking as bad.

"I don't understand what the fuck y'all problem is with each other anyway."

He came back in the kitchen, "I planned on talking to the nigga, but fuck that. He wants a problem, then I'm going to be the nigga that gives it to him. You Dior's blood, not mine. I don't give a fuck about you."

"That hoe ass nigga think I killed his pops, but I didn't have shit to do with that."

Bree's sister was just sitting there, staring back and forth between me and King, but her stare when she looked at him was of disgust. Something was telling me they knew each other before today.

"That's what I was trying to talk to you about bitch boy. I know you didn't kill him because my brother did. I'm a real nigga and I always right my wrongs. I was going to try to make amends with your dumb ass and let you know Marco was behind my pops getting killed. He was setting all of us up so that we would kill each other. He was on some real bitch nigga shit, but your bitch ass wants to be so hard that a nigga can't even talk civil with your dumb ass." I couldn't believe my fucking ears. I can't believe I had a snake in my circle for so long. I didn't even know what to say.

"My man, you can watch your fucking mouth. I am not that nigga you want to piss off. My bad nigga, shit, you were the same way. You should have come at a nigga like a real nigga, instead of trying to start a war you weren't going to win. On the strength of my sister, I came to help you, but you know we've been at each other's head."

He shook his head at me, then turned his head towards Adore, "And what the fuck you doing in my house?"

Bree snapped her head his way, "This is my sister and I invited her. Why, is that a problem?"

"I'm not even talking to you. Your sister on some sneaky shit, bringing her ass over here."

"Sneaky? Nigga, I didn't know Bree knew your hoe ass."

Dior looked at King with the evil eyes, "What the fuck you mean by that?" She looked at Adore, "Do you know him?"

Adore smirked, "I know him quite well, don't I Chance?"

It was too much going on in this bitch.

Bree looked at her sister, "Adore, don't start. You are not about to embarrass me."

"Fuck this nigga, Bree. I can't embarrass you when I'm not doing shit."

"Shit, yeah, I fucked a few times, but me and my fiancé had split, so bitch don't try to flex up like I was trying to wife your thot ass."

She started laughing, "A few times? Nigga, we were playing house."

"Bitch, what house? You stay in a hotel, what the fuck?"

Bree stood up and put her hand on her hip, "Nigga, you can stop disrespecting my sister. What the fuck you got going on? I don't give a fuck about all that, but disrespecting her is what you not gone do. And Adore, I hope you didn't bring your hoe ass over here to be messy and start shit."

"Bitch, I didn't even know you knew these folks, and I definitely didn't know he was with that bitch."

She had my sister fucked up. Dior stepped around Chance, "Bitch, I advise you to watch your mouth. You in my shit and you definitely don't want these problems. "Bree, you better let your sister know I have no problems putting a bitch on her ass."

"Nah, your sister knew what she was doing coming over here, she was being messy.

"So Bree, you on these motherfuckers' side now? Well how about you tell Dakota about you fucking his friend." Everybody's jaw dropped. How could she do something like that to her sister?

Me and Bree looked at each other, but my look was more of an evil and hurt look. "What friend Bree? You get down like that?"

"Dakota, let me explain…"

"Fuck that, you should have been told me. You foul ma, foul as fuck." I got up and walked off before I choked the shit out of her. Here I was trying to change for this hoe, and she smashing my homies. Bree shot Adore the death look and broke down in tears.

I heard Chance yelling at Adore, "Bitch, you a legit, messy ass thot. I would never want you."

"Nigga please, if I was being messy, I would have come in this bitch turned up. I didn't know we were coming to your house. Hell, I didn't even know my sister knew you. Don't try to pipe up on me like I was just a random fuck because if I was, I wouldn't be pregnant by your simple ass. BOOM NIGGA! NOW THAT'S SOME MESS FOR YOUR ASS." If looks could kill, she would be a dead ass bitch because everybody shot a menacing look her way. King was about to say something when their doorbell rang. *Who the fuck could that be?* I followed Dior to the door and I wasn't prepared for the person on the other side.

She opened the door and I grew angry, "What the fuck are you doing here?"

Chapter 13

Moe:

A bitch had been out of commission for quite some time, but I'm back and I'm popping like never before. I honestly thought I was dead when that nigga Marco shot me, but LOOK AT GOD, he gave me another chance. I fought so hard when I was in that coma because I had unfinished business to handle. Chance was a fool if he thought for one second I would allow him to keep Christian from me so that he could raise him with that bitch Dior. Fuck him, I just wanted my son. I understood his reasoning behind Christian not seeing me, but I had given him two weeks to come through and he failed, so now it was time to take matters into my own hands. He even switched Christian's school, but of course I found out what school he attended. I just hoped that my plan worked. That was the exact reason I was at his school now and I would explain everything to him.

"Hello, my name is Monique Baker and I am here to see Christian McCray."

"Are you a relative of the parents because I don't see your name on the list?"

"I am his mother, is that relative enough for you?" This bitch was pissing me off with all the questions.

"Ma'am, I'm sorry, but our documents say otherwise. Now I can call his father and if he says it is ok, then I will allow you to see him, but if not, I will have to ask you to leave."

"No, you don't have to do that, I will just see him some other time." Shit, that didn't go as planned, but I was going to see my damn son. I went back out to my car and sat there until it was time for him to get out of school, since he would be getting out in an hour. I sat in my car and jammed to the music, while I waited. Six o'clock finally rolled around and I saw a nice all white Audi pull in. A nice shaped woman got out and I noticed it was that bitch Dior. I hated her so much because that bitch was basically living my life. She went into the building and I got out of my car and started walking towards the entrance. After five minutes, she finally came out and stopped in her tracks when she saw me.

"I don't want any trouble, I just want to see Christian." He looked at me and grabbed a tighter grip on her hand.

"Come here Christian. Baby, it's mommy, don't be scared." She gave me an evil stare.

"Moe, what are you doing here? I thought that you and Chance agreed to give this situation some time."

"I gave his ass time. This is my son, y'all cannot keep him from me." She tilted her head to the side and put her hand on her hip.

"Listen up bitch, and listen good. Don't bring your ass up here trying to call the shots after the shit you pulled. Yes, he is your son, but you damn sure weren't acting like it. You the same chick that left him for months and had everybody thinking your hoe ass was dead. You a whole idiot out here. Go home Moe, you looking pretty bad."

"Oh bitch, don't get cute. I said I didn't want no problem, but you pushing it. It's all good though, I will be seeing y'all in court."

"Don't make a fool of yourself Moe. Do you honestly think you could win a court case? What the fuck do you have? Enough of all this though, I have already said too much in front of MY SON! Enjoy your sad ass day." She walked off and it took everything in me not to throw something at that bitch's head. I was trying to do things the adult way, but they had Monique Lashae Baker fucked up if they thought this shit was going down. I got in my car and drove off with no destination. I called Chance's phone because he was about to hear it.

"Yo, what the fuck Moe? Why are you going to Christian's school, acting stupid and shit?"

"Damn, your little chia pet didn't waste no time, huh? I want to get my son, Chance. Why are y'all keeping him from me? I am his mother, not that bitch." I was beyond livid. Who does shit like this? True enough, me running away played a big part in this, but I was trying to clean up my mistakes. I couldn't stomach the thought that I had to live without my son again.

"Fuck that, Moe. Give me time or you can forget the shit. You can't run in and out of his life whenever the fuck you please, bitch it doesn't work like that," he hung up. I burst out in tears because I was hurt. I felt destroyed. This was not over and they were going to regret fucking with me.

Dior:

It seemed like every time I took a step forward, I got knocked ten steps back. My mind had so many thoughts roaming through and I didn't know whether I was coming or going. My dinner turned out to be a complete disaster, and all I could think about was that night when I opened my door.

Sunday:

"What the fuck are you doing here?" My dad had shown up after over eight years and I wasn't the least bit happy to see him.

"Is that any way to talk to your father? I come in peace."

"Peace is what you will not get. The fuck you coming to my sister's doorstep for like you just been around and we invited your ass? Where you been nigga, didn't you leave us? We've been living good, no thanks to you or our whack ass mama." Dakota was giving it to his ass as I just stood there, staring. I had nothing to say. I didn't want to remember him and I damn sure didn't want to see him."

"I came to tell both of you some bad news."

"Wait, how do you know where I live?"

"Just because I haven't been around doesn't mean I haven't been keeping tabs on my children. Something terrible has happened and what other way to tell you than face to face."

"Ok Roberto, speak. I see your mouth moving, but you ain't saying shit." It would be a cold day in hell before we

called this man anything other than his name. That was something he should have stayed around and earned. He told us that our mother's body was found chopped into pieces and they found different parts of her body in two different rivers. How the hell did that happen? The bigger question was, who could do something like that?

That conversation was one that would haunt me until my dying days. That whole night was a disaster. On top of my dad's news, I had just been informed that Chance was sleeping with Bree's sister and got her pregnant. I was pissed to say the least, but then again, I couldn't really be too mad because we were separated when it happened. I would just have to put on my big girl panties and deal with it. Besides, who even knew if it was really his baby. He made his bed and now he would have to lay in it. I was over all the drama in my life. I just wanted to move on from it all and be happy. To do that, I knew sooner or later I would have to talk to Moe. I hated the situation at hand and wished it wasn't true, but she was my sister and I had to be an adult and tell her. It took everything in me not to be petty and burst her bubble when she pulled that shit at Christian's school, but as a woman, I understood her pain. I was going to be woman enough to allow her to see Christian and tell her about our mother. The first thing I needed to do was talk to Dakota about our mother and his situation with Chance.

Me: Hey bro, are you at the condo or Bree's house?

Dakota: I'm in the streets, what up?

Me: Meet me at the condo in twenty.

Dakota: Make it forty- five, I got some shit to handle right quick.

Me: Cool...

His forty-five meant an hour, so I dropped the kids off at Jas' and went to get me something to eat. I was so happy for her that she found someone that genuinely cared about her. It's not too many niggas that would mess with a pregnant female, so she pretty much lucked up. I pulled up to Dakota's condo and sat in my car until I saw him pull in. After waiting for an hour and twenty minutes, his ass finally arrived. I got out of the car and went to his car.

"Damn, I thought I was going to have to put out an amber alert, took your black ass long enough." We started walking towards the elevator since he stayed on the 16th floor.

"Shut the hell up, retarded ass girl. What the hell you wanted to meet me for anyway, interrupting my money and shit?" I walked in and sat on his couch, while he went to the kitchen to fix us a drink. I could tell he never stayed here because everything was exactly how it was the last time I came.

"I haven't talked to you since the dinner and I wanted to know how you felt about Roberto popping back up and what he said about Mommy." I knew better than to ask him this because my brother's heart turned cold the day my daddy left, and he hasn't been right since. Then my mother left and he really stop giving a fuck. I believe that's where his issue with women came to play.

"Shitt, how a nigga supposed to feel? In my eyes, them motherfuckers died years ago sis. I won't sit here and act like I'm all sad because Shan got killed. I mean look at the shit she did for a living, not to mention she abandoned us to pursue killing people. You reap what you sow. And Pops, that nigga not a man and he damn sure ain't my daddy, so a nigga still feeling quite lovely. I wouldn't have given a fuck if he was in the river right along with her dumb ass. I will continue to sleep comfortably every night. How you feel?"

I didn't understand how none of this affected him, not even a little bit. I mean at the end of the day, these were once our parents. "It does bother me a little that we were on bad terms and now she is dead before we could fix it. Roberto was still my dad at the end of the day and I had forgiven him for my past."

"Females too got damn forgiving. Fuck that and fuck them. Ain't no reconciling coming from me."

"You are so heartless Dakota. So I guess me mentioning trying to be cordial with Chance is a no go also, right?"

"Fuck no. Aye, what the fuck you trying to be DPhil the mediator or some shit? You know damn well I'm not being cordial with that nigga."

"He apologized Dakota. Damn, grow the fuck up." He shook his head no and cut his game on. "I'm thinking about telling Moe about Mommy and letting her know she is our sister."

He paused the game, then looked at me, "Yeah, you on some more shit. Since when you started trying to be the peacemaker?"

"When I decided life doesn't slow down and grew up, you should try it. But anyway, I'm about to go pick up the kids." I slapped him on the back of the head and walked out. That didn't go as planned, but my brother had to stop holding all these grudges.

Chapter 14

Chance:

This little bitch Adore would come around with her bullshit when me and my baby decide to work shit out and mess things up. I had been cut that hoe off completely. I almost pissed on myself when I saw her ass standing in my damn kitchen, talking to my fiancé like she belonged there. Now she claiming she pregnant and the fact that it might be mine pisses me off. I knew there was a huge chance it probably was because the last time we fucked, the rubber broke. Dior didn't go off like I thought she would and to be honest, that shit kind of scared me. I needed to talk to Adore about this baby situation because as much as I was against abortions, I didn't want her bearing my child. I stopped by my club I had built to make sure everything was going to fall through for my grand opening next week. My phone started ringing, it was Chasity.

"What up Chas, you good?"

"Umm, hey bro. No, Cali wants to talk to you, she got into a little trouble."

"Trouble? She got my number just like you do, so why didn't she call?"

"She is in jail and scared to call you. I told her she needed to call so that we can get her a lawyer, but she is just scared you will judge her." I knew for a fact I didn't hear her right. Ain't no way in hell Cali was in jail. She never got in any trouble.

"What you just say to me Chas? She what?"

"She is in jail for drug trafficking. She was pulled over by the cops and they searched her car."

I had to pull over on the side of the road. I was pissed, I was hurt, I was disappointed.

"WHAT THE FUCK YOU MEAN DRUG TRAFFICKING? WHERE THE FUCK SHE AT?"

"Rice St." I don't know what type of shit Cali was on, but she was going to catch hell from me. I knew that sorry ass excuse of a boyfriend she was with had something to do with this shit and I was going to get to the bottom of it.

"Yo, where is Mama? WHEN THE FUCK DID SHE GET LOCKED UP?" I was doing 120 on the dash, headed to Bankhead. There was no way in hell my little sister was staying in there. I was not the type to step foot in the jail because I hated the pigs, but I had to put all that to the side.

"Mommy is in Florida with her boyfriend and she won't answer the phone. Cali got locked up Sunday night and Rue has been keeping me updated with everything. Chance, they denied her bond." My head was spinning. I didn't know whether I was coming or going. How could Cali be so fucking stupid.

"Aight, I'm going to handle it, and tell her nigga he needs to hit my jack." I hung up before she could respond. If that nigga was the reason my sister was sitting in a jail cell, he was going to feel it. I pulled up to Fulton County and barely put the gear in park before I jumped out. I ran inside the building and to the help desk.

"How may I help you?"

"I need some information on the charges of Cali Frazier."

"She was brought in on drug charges and she has not been granted bond."

"Why the fuck did she not get a bond? This is her first offense."

"She plead guilty to possession of over a pound of marijuana. Her file has not been updated with her next court date, but visitation ends in thirty minutes if you wanted to see her."

"Yeah, let's do that." I filled out the necessary paperwork and was on my way to the visitation room. I sat by the phone and waited for them to bring Cali out. She came out and when she came to where I was, I could literally see her heart beating out of her chest.

"DON'T GET SCARED NOW, SIT THE FUCK DOWN," I yelled through the glass that separated us. She did as she was told and picked up the phone on her side.

"Chance, please let me explain…I—"

"Explain what? Ain't shit to explain besides the fact that you made a stupid fucking decision because you want to be a ride or die bitch so fucking bad. You look like a damn fool sitting your ass up in here, knowing damn well that shit wasn't yours."

"You don't get it Chance. I know why I did what I did and you have no right to come down here judging me. I'm a grown ass woman."

"You riding for a nigga that's probably laid up with the next bitch right now, instead of trying to get you the fuck out of here. Sometimes being ride or die not worth it Cali, but your "GROWN ASS" don't see that. Let me ask you something though, if that nigga cared about you, why is it that you need me to get you a lawyer?" She sat there with tears in her eyes and a big ass lump in her throat. I hit a nerve and I didn't give a fuck because right now, she needed tough love.

"You right big bro. I should have never gotten myself in this predicament, but Rue would never leave me hanging. I told him stay out of this situation because he already has a lot going on with this fucked up ass system. If you don't want to get me a lawyer, I will just have to sit here and ride it out." I shook my head because I didn't know who this was in front of me. This was not my little sister because my sister was smarter than this, but I guess love will make you do some crazy shit.

"Where that nigga at, and don't fucking lie? I will have my lawyer get right on your case, but I'm going to holla at that nigga." She started crying harder because she knew I was pissed and when I get pissed, I make the city bleed.

"He is usually at the studio around this time. The studio is next to the Chevron on Peachtree. Chance, please don't hurt him." The guard came and took her and I was headed to pay her lil bitch boy a visit.

Cody:

I was mentally fucked up from all the shit that went down the other night. Bree ain't said shit to me about fucking none of my homeboys, so I've been keeping my distance from her ass. Dior was a damn fool if she thought I was supposed to feel any kind of pain for my mother being dead and my dad popping back in the picture. I went through a lot of shit that Dior, nor anybody else knew, and I was the reason my pops left for good in the first place.

Ten years ago:

I was hanging with Drake at the basketball court after school, like we always did. Mom was at work and I had not seen my dad in over two years. He was always in and out of our lives, but me being the nigga that I was, I didn't give a fuck. Dior was over Auntie Rosetta's house for the weekend. After gambling on the dice for about three hours and taking everybody's bread, I was legit tired. I was only eleven, but I was a hot head at heart, and nothing was more important to me than getting money. Even though I was so young, there was nothing that I had not done. I had already caught my first body and I had the best marijuana around to be a young nigga. I had been selling weed since I hit middle school and didn't plan on stopping no time soon. I was walking home when I saw my dad getting out of the car with the nigga Blue the connect, and I got mad because I knew my dad was up to no good. I waited until I knew he was in the house good and settled, before I went in. As I entered the house, I overheard him on the phone with someone talking about my sister.

"Yeah, she's not here right now, but I will have her delivered to you, and the price for her is twenty-five thousand dollars. If anybody finds out that I was trying to trade my daughter to get out of debt, I would be a dead man." The nigga

was laughing like what he just said wasn't wrong. I stepped around the corner and charged at him. Now he was much bigger than me, seeing that I was barely a teenager, but that didn't stop me. I didn't play about my sister and anyone that tried to bring harm her way, was as good as dead. I punched him repeatedly in the rib until he doubled over in pain, then two pieced his ass and he fell. I pulled out my glock and pointed it at him.

"I want you to get the fuck out and never come back. I won't tell anybody what I heard, but if you even attempt to come back around, I won't hesitate to plant a hot one in your head."

"Son, it's not what you think..."

"I'm not your motherfucking son. No father would auction off his daughter for his own selfish needs, get the fuck out." I never disrespected my pops. I mean how could I, I looked up to him, until now. He left and I hadn't seen him since.

The fact that his punk ass came around made me want to hurt his ass more. I wasn't always this cold hearted ass nigga, but my parents not being able to love me and be there like a parent should, forced me to be the way I am. I was slowly changing into the man I needed to be, but one thing that will never change' I will never trust anybody. It's always been me and my sister since we were thirteen years old. My mom's trifling ass left us to fend for ourselves and my dad tried to pimp out my sister, my life was all fucked up. The shit with King was real fucked up. I had thought about what Dior said and this shit was blowing me. We been beefing and trying to kill each other for nothing. I felt a little bad about him having to kill his own brother, not to mention, a nigga that was eating with me. I sparked up a blunt and just let my thoughts take me away. In the past two years, I had been through so much and never had anybody I could vent to when shit got hectic. Up until I met Bree, I was lost as fuck because I had no guidance on how to treat a woman. She didn't give up on a nigga though and I appreciate that shit more than she knew. I know I put her through so much from different bitches to the disrespect that she endured daily because of me, but she remained solid. Bree ain't never betrayed me and that alone spoke volumes. I had even been thinking about asking her to marry a nigga. Me and my sister not as close as we were, and that's because I distanced myself from her when she started fucking with King. Now I'm trying to better myself for my kids, and that has to start with me getting that bond back with my sister. If she wants me to reconcile with the nigga King, so be it. I didn't want karma to attack my kids for shit I did. I had a daughter coming and if a nigga treated my daughter the way I treated these females out here, I will have to body his ass, no ifs, ands, or buts about it. That goes for my niece too. I want her to grow up with my kids also and have that close bond with me. I planned on doing shit the right way when it came to my family. My phone rang, bringing me out of my thoughts and it was my baby Bree.

"What up bae?"

"Dakota, it's time, my water just broke."

Chapter 15

Adore:

Drama, drama, drama, is all I've been dealing with lately. It wasn't my intentions to expose my sister like that, but she pissed me off when she took everybody else's side and started ganging up on me. If she was still mad about it, that was her business, and I didn't give a fuck. Chance has been getting on my last damn nerves about this whole baby situation. I found out yesterday that I was nine weeks. There wasn't anything to be mad about because it happened and it is what it is. What he's not going to do is keep nagging me about it though. I couldn't believe I ended up at his house. This world was too got damn small. He asked me could he come over so that we could talk about the situation at hand, and I had a few hours to spare before I met my client, so I told him to stop by.

"So, what are we going to do about this baby? I don't mean to be rude or nothing, but I don't want no baby with you ma. I don't even know your ass like that and you seem a bit messy, since you showed up at my crib."

"Hold up, let's be clear about something. I didn't know I was coming to your stupid ass house for the last got damn time and I definitely didn't know you even knew my sister. You never told me shit about your little bitch, except the fact that you had one, so you can kill the bullshit you talking. As far as this baby goes, I still have my options open. You act like it's a privilege to be pregnant by your hoe ass. Your dick big, but you barely even know what to do with it, so don't be mad at me because your sorry ass sex caused the condom to break." I was lying my ass off right about now because his sex was magnificent. I had never had pipe laid on me like that, but I would be damned if I told him that and boosted his ego.

He started chuckling, "Is that right? I'm going to spare your thot ass because I know that's what you hoes do when y'all get mad because a nigga ain't giving y'all the dick no more. Y'all turn bitter. As for my wife, you can watch your fucking mouth. Nobody disrespects her and I could guarantee you she would beat the shit out of you, but we not on that. I came to talk about this baby and that is the only reason I am here. Now I'm getting my shit together with my lady and we don't need any distractions, so what's it going to be?"

This nigga had to be on some serious drugs to think he could come up in here and call me a hoe, then try to demand some shit. I didn't want to deal with this the rest of my life because fucking with him, I would probably catch a case.

"You know what, you just like the rest of these niggas out here. Now she your wife, but when she wasn't fucking with you, you were all laid up, pillow talking and shit. I'll tell you what, you can give me the money and I will take care of it and you can stay the fuck away from me." I was hurt, this was somebody I had developed feelings for. He wasn't the real nigga he portrayed to be because a real nigga would accept his responsibility.

"Nah ma, I'm a street nigga and I'm smarter than that. You about to sit your ass right here and make that phone call and I will take you to the appointment when it's time. You had to have known you weren't about to play me like that."

"You think you a real nigga too, don't you? Well, you are far from it. You just going to kill your responsibility like it's nothing?"

"I know I'm a real nigga. You weren't supposed to get pregnant in the first place, but the rubber broke. You not the type of female I would have kids with and I know now that you would be one of those bitches that cause problems, and I don't play like that. Look how fast you gave me the pussy, you have too many hoe tendencies."

"Ok, get the fuck out. I will let you know when my appointment is, I have nothing else to say to you." This was straight bullshit. I've never been a hoe, so I was not about to sit and listen to him dog me out like I was just a worldwide hoe. I wanted him out of my face like yesterday.

"I said make the call and I will gladly leave." I called Summit Abortion Clinic and set my appointment for this Friday.

I didn't want to kill an innocent child because it didn't ask to be here, but fuck that, I will repent later, this nigga had to go. The sooner I did it, the better.

"I will be here Friday to take you to handle that, and don't try nothing stupid. I'm sorry shit had to be like this, I really am, but wifey comes first. When you get your own nigga, you will understand." He started laughing as he walked out of the door. I barely let him make it all the way out before I slammed the door, hitting him gently with it. I hopped in the shower to get myself ready for this client I was meeting. Based on her profile, she had a lot going on in her life and I knew it was about to be one hell of a session. I threw on my Akris Punto pants suit with a pair of Red Bottoms. I flat ironed my hair so it was bone straight, and put on a pair of hoop earrings. I grabbed my Prada handbag and left out. It took me about twenty minutes to get to the office that I was assigned to be working at and I was impressed. My temporary assistant, Judith, told me that my client was already here and ready for her session. I walked into the office and she was much prettier than what I imagined. I mean her profile photo did her no justice.

"Hello, I am Dr. Adore Watkins, nice to meet you."

"Nice to meet you too. I am Monique Baker."

Jas:

Those motherfuckers have too much going on for me. Lil mama was foul for doing that to her sister, but thots never prosper, and she should have been told Dakota about fucking Drake. I've known about it, but that was none of my business, and I'm far from one of those hating hoes that expose hoes for their benefit. I wish I had some popcorn for all that drama, I thought I was on Jerry Springer. Me and Carlos kicked back and watched everything unfold. When I tell you Carlos is heaven sent, that is what I mean. He never ceases to amaze me and I appreciated him so much for that. Who said pregnant bitches couldn't pull niggas again? They lied, I know that much. We have been kicking it so heavy and I enjoy every moment. He wines and dines your girl something serious. Just when I thought I was broken and couldn't be fixed, LOOK AT GOD, he showed up and showed out. The other night when we were at Dior's for dinner, my childish ass baby daddy thought he was going to come for my babe, but I shut that shit down quick. I didn't even understand why he was even checking for me. That same night, he was texting me, asking me was I fucking him, but I didn't think it was his business. Me being Ms. Petty Betty, I told his ass yes. That was as far away from the truth as it could get. I had not bust this fat cat open in eight months, and my hormones were at an all-time high. Los been eating the hell out of the cat though. Dakota was a beast with his tongue, but he wasn't fucking with Los on any level, even if my baby wrote the instructions down. That nigga kept my orgasms on panic mode each time, no lie. I couldn't believe all the shit that happened at my girl's house though, and I know she was hurt about the situation with Chance. That shit crazy that he ended up getting Bree's sister pregnant. These niggas ain't shit and stay passing out their dick like it's charity. My heart was hurting for my dog because if anybody knew how she felt about her Chance, it was me. My text notifications went off and I had two messages, one from bae and one from Dakota. I opened Dakota's first.

Baby daddy: *Come to the hospital, Bree is in labor.*

Now I didn't know what the hell would make him think I wanted to come to the hospital. I could see if my baby girl was already here, but she is not, so what purpose would me going there serve.

Me: *What am I coming there for?*

Baby daddy: *Come on Jas, don't be like that. Y'all supposed to be talking anyway, so get your ass up here...please.*

Me: *Ugh, alright damn.*

I didn't know what this was about, but I guess I would be heading there. I opened my message from Los.

Babe: *I miss you sweet cheeks. (kissy face)*

Me: *Oh how I miss you too (Sad face)*

He was calling me while I started to get dressed. I was not going to tell him where I was headed, but fuck it, we kept it real with each other at all times.

"You don't miss me girl, stop lying."

"Yes I do, Papa, you just don't know."

"Yeah, I bet. I just left your big head ass not too long ago. What you up to though?"

"Nothing much, getting dressed. Baby daddy's other baby mama went in labor, and for some strange reason, I was asked to come up there."

"Is that right? Don't be letting that nigga munch on my sweet stuff. He lost when he let you slip, so tell him keep it that way." I was laughing because my baby could be so jealous sometimes.

"You have absolutely nothing to worry about. What time you coming over, and it better not be late." I rolled my eyes and tilted my head to the side, as if he was right in front of me.

"Nah, not late at all. Matter of fact, pack you a hoe bag, you coming with me for the rest of the week."

"Straight like that huh? You just going to tell me instead of ask."

"Hell yeah, I wear the pants around this muhfucka, remember that."

"Whatever, boy. Bye, I will call you later."

"Alright ma, be safe out there."

"No, you be safe." I hung up the phone. I was really falling for Los and hoped he planned on catching me. We had not put a title on what we were, but he was mine and I always got what I wanted. I got dressed in a pair of Nike jogging pants and the shirt to match. I put on a pair of Air Force Ones and put my hair in a neat ponytail and was ready to go. I had been driving Los' Dodge Durango SR/T and had no plans of giving it back. I hopped in the truck and was on my way to the hospital. So many thoughts roamed my brain about my life since I got pregnant. Here I was, going on twenty- five weeks pregnant, and already moved on from my baby daddy. True enough, me and Dakota were never really in a relationship, but we were very close to it. I regretted every day that I dedicated to his ungrateful ass and hate him for the way he made me. I wish I had family I could vent to, but I have nobody. My mother died from cancer six years ago and my brother, Jamir, was killed right after I graduated high school. Dakota was a breath of fresh air for me, until I gave him my kitty and his ass ain't been right ever since. He lied about everything and hurt me to the core, making my heart cold. Then Los comes along and shows me what it feels like to have a real man. He introduced me to real and now I hated lames, exact reason why I hated Dakota. I bet my daughter was going to come out looking just like his ass. Nah for real, Carlos might just be it for me, but only time will tell. I pulled up to the hospital, and prayed nobody was on no bullshit.

Chapter 16

Dior:

"Christian, bring Cayleigh's diaper bag off the couch and get your jacket."

We were headed to a festival at the daycare where Christian goes. School had started back and I had two classes later on. The weird thing about it, I was excited to be back in school because the drama that had been surrounding my life seemed like it would never end. School would take my mind from it all.

We stay on the front lines

Yeah but we're still here after the bomb drops

We go so hard we lose control

The fire starts then we explode

When the smoke clears we dry our tears

Only in love and war

Chance was calling, so I ran to answer the phone.

"Hello?"

"What time is the little festival shit?"

"We are headed out the door now, where are you?"

"I'm picking up my last bag and I will meet y'all up there. What we eating tonight?"

"Y'all eating take-out, you know I have class today."

"Damn, I forgot bae. Alright, I'll see y'all in a minute."

Things with me and Chance were slowly progressing back to how they were, and I was more than happy about it. We still had a few things to work on, starting with this Adore situation. I told him I would stay out of it, but I don't want no shit from neither of them. I was pissed about it, but I couldn't show it because that was before we got back together. Only thing that bothered me was I didn't know if she was the reason we had broken up in the first place. He said it was somebody else, but I knew better. I just wasn't the type that would take a nigga back and constantly throw what he did in his face. I would just let the past be the past, until further notice. I wasn't mad at Bree about the situation because I seriously feel that the news had shocked her just as much as everyone else. I was happy Dakota was getting his shit together with her because she wasn't all that bad. I had let go of the grudge I had with her about the Drake situation because it wasn't worth the stress. I was working on becoming a better me and holding grudges wasn't part of the process. I just hoped I could keep my sanity with all the nonsense that constantly came my way.

I was told that my mother's body was cremated of course, and I had not seen Roberto since the day he delivered the news. I wasn't surprised her previous life had caught up with her to say the least. I still found it hard to forgive my father for the things he had done to me when I was younger. I was so insecure with myself when I was younger because I didn't have a father's love like everyone else, and it hurt me on a daily basis. I took my trust issues from my father out on the men that came into my life.

Twelve *years old:*

Daddy had picked me up from school and said that we were spending some father daughter time. I knew Dakota would be mad with me because he had to stay in school. He told me we were going to his friend's house so that I could play with his daughter. When we got there, I didn't see any children and the house looked so bad that I was scared to walk in. Daddy and his friend were the cleanest people in here, and I felt like they didn't belong. It smelled so bad. Like when I was younger and used to wet the bed, the smell was all so familiar. I didn't see any little girls. I only saw two people that looked homeless, leaned up against the wall, halfway sleep. The curtains in this house were nonexistent and the walls were no longer white. I didn't understand why Daddy had bought me to a place like this, until I heard his friend start talking.

"OK, so I will clear your debt with me for about thirty minutes, is that cool?"

"That will work perfectly."

His friend grabbed my hand and told me to come with him. Him and Daddy took me to one of the rooms in the back and the mattress was very dirty and the cotton was coming out of the sides. He told me to sit down and started unzipping my pants. I pushed his hand away and Daddy popped me.

"Princess, he is not going to hurt you, just be still." I couldn't believe Daddy was letting this happen. His friend started touching and massaging my private area and Daddy just stood there, when he was supposed to be protecting me. His friend started licking on my private part and I couldn't stop crying. I cried until it was over and we got in the car headed home.

"Princess, keep this between us, ok? Be a good girl and I will give you an allowance every week if you don't tell." Daddy let that man do bad things to me until I was eleven, and he just disappeared.

"Mommy Dior, why are you crying?"

I had promised myself I would never think about those years of my life again because those years ruined me. I was crying my eyes out and I knew I needed to seek help before this destroyed me.

"Oh nothing baby, Mommy had something in her eyes."

I was still holding the pain from so many years ago. I never told anyone about it, but it was time I told someone, and maybe that weight would be lifted off my shoulders. We pulled in to the daycare and stayed at the festival until it was over. I called Jas to drop the kids off, but she didn't answer. My phone started ringing and it was Dakota saying that Bree was in the hospital in labor. I hit a U and headed that way. I wouldn't miss my nephews being born for nothing in the world. I got to the hospital and got the shock of my life, Chance was there with Adore.

Bree:

I was still pissed off with my sister for that bullshit she pulled at Dior's house. I was more so mad at myself for confiding in her fake ass. She had been calling me, but I had nothing to say to her. Dakota has been around, but he was giving me the silent treatment. I went ahead and told him about me and Drake and told him that was before we got serious. He was still distant from me, but he was slowly calming down. I was at home, cleaning my house from top to bottom, when I felt a sharp pain shoot down my back. I tried to continue doing what I was doing, until a pain much worse shot down my spine, causing me to fall on my knees. I thought I was peeing on myself, until it hit me that my water had broken. I got my phone out of my pocket and called 911, and it took them little to no time to get there. I called Dakota so that he could meet me there. It had been sixteen hours and I was still sitting here, waiting for these bad ass little boys to make their grand entrance. Dakota had his head rested on my stomach, rubbing it in hopes to soothe the pain, but the shit was not working at all. "Dakota, this is all your fault and I hope you are happy because we will not be doing this again."

He smirked, "Shitt, I want three more. I'm trying to promote my own football team." I started laughing and another contraction came. I was still stuck at five centimeters and it was pissing me off. I was ready to get this over with. A knock came at the door and Jasmine walked in. I immediately got mad.

"What are you doing here? Dakota, I know damn well you didn't tell your side bitch to come up here for the birth of my kids."

"Yo, chill out Bree, damn. This shit is bigger than that. Nobody on no sneaky shit and its time both of y'all realize these kids will be siblings, whether you like it or not. We all grown as fuck, so the beef needs to be put to rest today. Y'all shouldn't have even been going through all this shit anyway, the beef should have been with me. I told her come up here because I wanted to talk to y'all and kill this shit."

"You picked a hell of a time to do this. I'm in labor, what the fuck? You think I'm trying to have girl talk and pop popcorn right now. No nigga, I don't." He really turned up with this one. True enough, we shouldn't be having these issues with one another, but right now, Jasmine was the last thing I had on my mind. She took it upon herself to have a seat in the corner and scroll through her phone.

She looked up at me, "Listen Bree, he is right. I can't believe my damn self that I showed up here, but I'm here. We have to get this shit together for the sake of these children and be adults about the situation. I don't want to limit his time with his daughter because I'm skeptical about him bringing her around you, and I'm pretty sure you feel the same." The contractions started coming back to back. I couldn't believe these two were in here trying to be therapists right now, while I'm in labor. This shit could have waited. Jasmine stepped out when the doctor came in. I was now ten centimeters and I was pissed that it was now too late to get the epidural.

"Ok Ms. Aubree, on your next contraction, I want you to push." Dakota was holding my hand through it all. After ten minutes of pushing, one of my boys came out. I was exhausted, but I knew I had one more to go. Two minutes later, I pushed my last baby out. Dakota cut the umbilical cords, then they took them to clean and weigh them. I was now a mother to two baby boys. We named them Damari Neshawn Baker and Deimo Neshawd Baker. Damari weighed 6lbs 10oz and Deimo weighed 6lbs 6oz. I fell in love the moment the doctor placed them in my arms.

Dakota kissed me on the forehead and said, "We complete now bae." I was in heaven and my king and two princes were more than enough for me. I wouldn't trade this moment for anything. Dakota and Jasmine were right, there was no longer a need to hold a grudge when Dakota was in the wrong. If I could forgive him, then I could forgive her.

"Babe, tell Jasmine to come her for a second." He gave me back the boys and left out of the room. I sat there and stared at my boys, they were so perfect. I only carried them because they looked nothing like me. Only thing they took from me was my eyes. They didn't get those beautiful eyes like their father, but they were perfect. Dakota and Jasmine walked back in and she looked at the boys and smiled. "Can I hold one of them? What are their names?" I handed her Damari. "Damari and Deimo. I told Dakota to come get you so that we could talk. I don't want our issues to affect these kids in the long run. We will never be friends, but we could at least attempt to be cordial. I just need to know if there are still any feelings lingering for Dakota?"

She looked at me with a blank facial expression, "I will be honest with you, there will always be feelings for Dakota, he was my first everything, but do I still want him? No, I don't. I have someone that appreciates me and worships the ground I walk on. You can have those issues, I had enough. The only thing I want with Dakota is a friendship and to co-parent our daughter the right way. I don't want nothing more and nothing less." As much as I didn't want to, I believed her, but for now, I would give her the benefit of the doubt. Dakota just sat there, holding Deimo, and the bond I saw between them was amazing. There was another knock at the door and Dior walked in and she didn't look too happy.

Chapter 17

Chance:

It seemed like every time I tried to move ahead with Dior, Adore would come and fuck it all up. I was headed to the festival, when Adore started calling back to back, and told me she was at the hospital. I know she was scheduled to get an abortion Friday, so it shocked me when she called with an emergency. I turned around and headed to the hospital to see what was going on. The doctor told her that she had lost the baby and I felt a little bad about it. True enough, she was getting rid of it, but to actually go through the process of losing it was a whole different route. I wasn't no lame ass nigga that would leave her to deal with this alone, because when it all boiled down, it was just as much mine, as it was hers. I had no feelings whatsoever about her, but I would look like a sucker had I not shown up. We were standing in the hall, getting ready to leave, when Dior walked in with my kids. I felt my soul leave my body when I saw tears building up in her eyes, and Adore smiling.

"Bitch, you better wipe that stupid smirk off your face before I do it for you, and you really don't want that."

"I highly doubt that, play with it." I had to do something quick because I didn't want them fighting, especially not in front of the kids. With the way Dior was set up, she was about to pop off.

I started walking towards her and she held her hand up, "Nah, I'm good. Go back over there with your little poor whore. I will be just fine." I knew I was about to be in the doghouse all over again. "You're supposed to have been on your way to your family, but you up here posted with that bitch. Now I have kept quiet about this situation because you told me you took care of it, and I'm trying to change my ways, so why you up here Chance? What's up?"

"He came to make sure me and his unborn were good bitch, so how about you leave."

"Yo, shut the fuck up. Bae, it's not what it looks like, I swear."

She put her hand up and stepped around me, "Hold up lil bitch because it seems like you big mad. You mad at me like he was your nigga or something. Now I said I grew up off that petty shit, but I can pull my pettiness out right quick and beat that ass."

Adore thought it was funny and stepped a little closer.

"Bae, I was taking her to get an abortion Friday, but she lost it last night. I just came to make sure she was straight. I promise I wasn't on no fuck shit."

"You don't have to explain shit to her, especially when it comes to me."

"Ok bitch, that's it." Dior sat her purse on the counter and sat Cayleigh's car seat down, then tried to charge at Adore, but I grabbed her.

"No Dior, not in front of the kids, please. Please calm down, it's not worth it." Adore threw her hands up and turned to walk off.

"Get the fuck off of me. I'm so tired of you and the drama that comes with you. When does it end? I mean here I am, trying to change my ways so that we could move forward, but no, your ass still keeping secrets and shit. I am seriously tired Chance." It hurt a nigga bad as fuck seeing my baby cry like this in front of a bitch that probably caught a nut off of her pain. I was starting to feel like Dior would be better off without me. I had been so caught up in this situation I didn't even ask her why she was here.

"I'm sorry bae. I keep fucking up and I hate myself for it. I promise I'm going to get this shit together ma, I got to."

"Yeah ok, Chance. I have to go, my nephews were just born and me sitting here with you and this bird not doing nothing but pissing me off."

"Wait, what? Where is Bree? She didn't even call me," she stormed off towards the women's center. I forgot the bitch was even here. She just stood there and listened to everything; yeah, this bitch had to go.

I grabbed Cayleigh's seat and Christian's hand, "Go see about your people ma. I will take the kids and when you get home, we will talk."

"I'm sure we will. I believe we moved too fast when we got back together. I need to figure this shit out and decide if this is what we need." She walked off and I headed to the house. I wasn't accepting the fact that Dior had second thoughts on whether or not she wanted to be with me. I loved her too much. She will just have to accept me, flaws and all, like I accepted her. She gave me life and I would be damned if she took it from me. Dior was the air I needed to breathe. I ain't do shit, so leaving me was as far from an option as it would get. I had so much shit on my mind and nobody to vent to. My mom was damn near nonexistent, Chasity was acting weird, and Cali was in jail. I called my lawyer to see what the deal was on my sister. He was slipping not keeping me posted on her case.

"Yo, Beckford, what up nigga, what's the word?"

"It's not looking too good my man. The prosecutor working her case is an asshole and he is hard to break. The offer he put on the table is five, do one with four years' probation. I can try for one year under first offender, but it's not guaranteed."

"WHAT THE FUCK DO YOU MEAN five DO one? Nah nigga, I'm not going for that, and tell Cali don't budge on that deal. You better get off your ass and get something better or your ass is fired. I don't pay you to try shit nigga, I pay you to do it." This nigga had me fucked up if he thought he would just give up on my sister because shit got tough. That prosecutor didn't know who he was fucking with. I would body his ass before I let him send my little sister away.

Cody:

A nigga was happy as hell right about now. I was still on edge with Bree, but she finally told me the truth about everything. If that nigga Drake was still here, I would have beat his ass. I was fucked up that both of my right hand men were stabbing me in the back. I told Bree it would take some time, but I still wanted to be with my family. If I didn't love Bree before, I loved the fuck out of her ass now. I damn near passed out seeing her shit spread all wide like that. Ain't no way in hell that shit was supposed to open up like that. Seeing my sons enter this world gave me a whole new outlook on life and I want to cherish every moment. I was still a work in progress, but I had to tighten up for my baby and my kids. I was happy I was able to get her and Jas to come to some type of agreement, even though it wasn't all peaches and cream at first. I wanted to be there for my kids because my parents weren't there for me, and I don't want them to turn out fucked up like their daddy. I can't lie though, hearing Jas say she cared about that nigga she was with fucked with me on all types of levels. Yeah, it may sound selfish, but she was always supposed to want me. Dior walked in our room and I could tell something was bothering her.

"Aye sis, come holla at me in the hallway right quick."

We walked out of the room and she leaned against the wall. "What is it and what is Jas doing in there?"

"You were right sis. A nigga needs to change his ways, so I asked Jas to come up here. Bree was mad at first, but they set aside their differences and I thank God that shit didn't go left. Fuck all that though, what's going on with you, why you been crying?"

"Cody, my life is such a mess. It's so much bothering me I wouldn't know where to start. I'm in love with a nigga that my brother has beef with and I'm in too deep, but we just can't get right."

Listening to my sister pour her heart out for this nigga really bothered me. Regardless of how I felt about the nigga, I had to be there for her.

"Now you know I'm not Team Chance or whatever the nigga's name is, but you have to stop letting everybody else control how you feel. So what if I don't like him, that's who you love and I just have to deal with it. That's my niece's father and I would never be selfish and jeopardize their bond. Fuck me and how I feel, what matters is what Dior wants."

"It's not just that, this whole situation with Adore is getting the best of me. When I got here, I saw him here with her and even though she was carrying his child, it still bothered me. Bro, I swear I've been changing for the better, but I could really kill that hoe for doing this to my family."

"Dior, let me give you some game right now. You can't keep blaming her for his faults. As a recovering hoe, I know how the nigga feels. Niggas always think with their second head, then when shit gets tough, we want to ask our first head for advice. I don't like that nigga, but I know he loves you and those kids more than anything. You need to see where his head at, D. Don't let that nothing ass hoe ruin the empire you built. It's a fact that he was wrong for not letting you know the deal about him coming up here, but be honest, could you fuck with a nigga that made a baby and left his baby mama to handle shit on her own? Don't let this shit make you sweat sis, he was just being a man, regardless of the situation."

"I guess you right Cody. We just have to take it a day at a time. Let me find out you growing up nigga," she punched me in the arm and started laughing.

"There's the Dior I know. Nah, for real ma, get your shit back on track. You have to learn to let your past issues stay in the past."

"Thanks a lot big head. I knew I could talk to you if I couldn't talk to anybody else, even though we kind of drifted apart."

I could tell she took everything I told her in. Hell, I couldn't believe my damn self for taking up for this nigga. I'm a real nigga though and I was just telling my sister the truth. I knew I had to man up and get over this high school shit me and this nigga had going on. I gave my sister a hug and sent her on her way. There were positive vibes only in the room with my boys. I had decided that I would propose to Bree when all this shit boiled down. Right now, I just wanted to enjoy my family. I had a little business to take care of, so I had to leave for a few. I spent a couple more minutes with my family and hit the streets. I got mouths to feed and I couldn't do it sitting here. I'm ready to be out of the game and I had some loose ends before I made my exit. My family was all that mattered to me.

Chapter 18

Adore:

I came back to Georgia with the intentions of business and ended up with life changing drama. Me losing my baby triggered something in me that I buried so long ago. I was starting to believe I needed to be the one in the chair being seen by a psychologist, versus playing the role of one. My last session was the most sensitive and craziest one I have had yet.

"So Monique, what brings you in today?"

"Well, I have been through so much more than your average twenty-four-year-old. My problems started when I was young. When I was a few months old, my mother disappeared and I was told she was dead. I don't remember what she looked like, nor do I remember her name. I bounced around in different foster homes, being molested in each one, until I felt I was able to take care of myself. I have been pregnant more times than you can count by different guys, due to me prostituting my body to live. I felt so alone and betrayed because none of my family came for me. Five years ago, I fell in love with a man that showed me what it was to be loved. I rode for him, even when the riding got tough. I never betrayed him or anything. I got pregnant and I thought things would sprout into something better than what they were, but they only got worse. A lot of our problems came from his family hating me and not wanting him to be with me. He continuously told me that how they felt didn't matter, but I knew it was different. Then he met another woman and fell in love with her and forgot all about me. I met this guy that paid me to do bad shit and I ended up betraying the man that once loved me for someone that ended up constantly beating my ass. The guy ended up shooting me and I fell into a coma for almost two months. Now that I am home, they won't let me see my son and I am losing my mind. I can't sleep at night, I cry 24/7, and sometimes I just wish I would have died.

"How has that made you today?"

"I am bitter and all I think about is revenge. I am here because I don't want to be this way. I'm tired of being this bitter woman because people hurt me."

"The first step is admitting your wrongs and you have done that. You should let these people know about your past and how they played a role in your pain."

"I will try to do that. Thank you so much. Talking to you made me a feel a little better because I've never told anyone about my past. I think I will start with Chance, since he hurt me the most."

"Wait, what? Chance who?"

"McCray, do you know him?"

"Oh no, not at all."

Our conversation played over and over in my mind. I didn't feel like answering questions about how I knew Chance, he wasn't worth anymore of my time. He really pissed me the fuck off at that hospital, going against me for that bitch once again. I was so sick of that little spoiled brat and her bullshit. That was the main reason I cut her brake line in her car. The world would be a better place without Ms. Dior. Since I had done that, I was packing my bags back up to leave Georgia, and for good this time. The deed was done and I did what I came to do. I was leaving to start my life over and get away from all of this drama. I ran me some bath water and put bath beads in it so that I could relax before my flight. I lit a few candles, turned my Pandora on, and let the music take me away. My thoughts drifted off to my first love Cortez.

It was crazy how we had been apart for over three years and he still had a hold on me. I loved him more than I loved myself. Cortez gave me any and everything I asked for, no questions asked, but after a while it all came with a price. I dealt with different bitches, got my ass beat by him, and got three STD's and I still stuck around. I got pregnant and he left me high and dry with no explanation. He started telling everybody around that the baby wasn't his because I had cheated on him. A real fuck nigga indeed, huh. He ended up coming back and like a fool, I accepted him with open arms. He came home one night and I didn't have dinner ready, so he pounded on my face until he broke my jawbone. I paid over five thousand dollars to get my face reconstructed and nobody ever knew. The next morning, he took me to get an abortion and told me things would get better and that he wasn't ready for kids, but I knew better. Not even a month after I got my abortion, I found out he had a baby on the way and the girl was five months, having a little boy. That put the icing on the cake. I left him and never turned back.

I didn't know if I just attracted ain't shit niggas or if good dick made me weak and lost. Every nigga I came across dragged me, whether we were in a relationship or just friends with benefits. Ever since me and Cortez split, I kept my heart locked, but Chance had found the key. I couldn't help how I felt about him because he seemed so perfect. If he could love Dior, then he could learn to love me too. I was willing to do anything for him, even if it meant murder, but who was I kidding. I was seriously on the verge of giving up and that was why I planned on moving. Maybe distance would make the heart grow fonder. I'm just thinking out the box. Fuck Chance, I deserved better. Since he hurt me, I had to hurt his precious Dior.

Cali:

I had been locked up for over a month now and this shit was for the birds. I wanted so bad to take a real shower in a real bath tub. I wanted to get my hair slayed like I kept it, but being here kept me from everything. I have been in three fights since I have been here because the bitches think because I'm pretty as hell, they could try me. I had to beat a stud to sleep yesterday because she thought it was ok to grab at my kitty. I'm not with that gay shit. I don't play those type of games and would beat a bitch dead about my respect. I was missing Rue something serious and I hate there was nothing I could do about it. He kept money on my books and he came to visit me every now and then, but I always told him to stay away from here. I loved him so much, that's why I took this charge for him. His birthday is tomorrow and it's killing me because I can't turn up with him. We have always spent holidays and birthdays together. I have been calling Chasity all week and she has not been answering my calls, which was weird because she was the one keeping track of everything going on with my case. I had a meeting with my lawyer today to see what deals they had to offer to get me out of here.

"FRAZIER, STEP UP."

We headed down to the secluded visitation room, so that I could talk to my lawyer.

"What up Cali, how you holding up?"

"I'm good, what's up? Tell me some good news."

I wasn't expecting for Beckford to tell me they offered me five years, do one and four years of probation, but Chance told me not to take the offer. He said my brother told me to hold tight, he was going to get me out. I didn't know how the hell he was going to do that when I had no bond and my trial date was a month away. I just needed to get the hell out of here. The guard came and took me back to my cell and I couldn't wait for my phone call because I needed to talk to Chance and see what's up with Chasity. I hope everything was ok because this was a no go. They let me out of my cell to make a phone call and I dialed Chance's number.

"How you holding up in there sis?"

"I'm good. Small thing to a giant, just ready to come home."

"Yeah, I'm making moves to get you out of there. You denied that plea deal they offered you, right? Don't fall for that shit, we're going to get something better."

"Have you heard from Chas? She won't answer my calls and I was a little worried."

"Hell nah, I will stop by the crib when I get some time. I will have some information for you when I talk to you again. Keep your head up sis, you will be home soon. Love you."

"Love you too."

I hung up and called Rue while I still had a little time to spare, but he didn't answer. I don't know what the fuck is going on out there, but I will find out. I never had trust issues when it came to Rue because he gave me no reason to. Now that I have been stuck in here, everything comes off as suspicious to me. I felt alone and that was the worst way to feel. Here I am, sitting here on a charge for my nigga, and he's been acing shady lately. I had something for his ass. When it comes to my mother, I have not talk to her since I came back from Miami. I had nobody in here, so what was the point of me going home, so everybody could act like they missed me? I'm over all of this shit. Chas has not been the same for years and I was tired of that shit. I had rage on my mind. I felt like somebody was out to get me, I just didn't know who. I went back into my cell and wrote Rue a letter.

Dear Nye,

I don't know what the fuck is going out there, but you need to get at me. I have not seen, nor talked to you all week, so what's up? Don't you miss me? They offered me five years, do one, but I denied it. My trial date is coming up pretty soon and I would like to come home to my so-called man and be the way we were. You need to come see me Nyrue or we will have some problems. At first, you were riding for me, but you done switched up. Don't forget the real reason I'm here.

-Calz

These folks had me fucked up if they thought I would just sit back while they were out there parlaying and shit. I love Chance because I knew for a fact he was riding for his sister, too bad I couldn't say the same for Chas. My heart was hurting and when my heart hurts, I become eager to hurt someone else. I missed my family and I was tired of playing tough, it hurts. I tried to come up with different ways to keep my mind off the matter at hand, but kept coming up short.

"Hey, I know you," someone said from the cell across from me. "You Rue's little girlfriend, right?"

"Yeah, and who the hell are you?" I said with my arms folded over my chest.

"I'm Porsche, Rue's cousin."

A vivid memory came of her and damn she looked bad. She looked a lot different from what I remembered. "What happened to you?"

"Life. I have been here six months, but that's neither here nor there. Umm, how is that sister of yours?"

"Why you asking about my sister?"

She started laughing, "You must really love your sister, huh?"

"Of course. Look, stop beating around the bush, what's up?"

"Your sister been trying to fuck my cousin for years boo, he never told you?"

At that moment, I heard my heart break. How could Chas do something like this? No wonder she acted like she didn't want us together. Furthermore, how could he not tell me some shit like that. I didn't know how true this was, but I was damn sure going to find out, and one or both of them would pay for these tears.

Chapter 19

Dior:

I really enjoyed having that talk with my brother. It felt just like old times. We had been through so much and we should have never got to the place we were in. My nephews were drop dead gorgeous and I loved them as if they were my own. Bree wasn't a bad person at all and I think she was perfect for Dakota.

The past few weeks Drake had been crossing my mind a lot and I had to admit, I kind of missed him getting on my nerves. I think that Drake being gone forced Dakota to realize how short life really was. We never even got the chance to properly say goodbye because his family took him to Connecticut and had a private funeral. That really hurt us to the core because we all grew up together. His dad blamed us for his death and I accepted it because a part of me felt like this was our fault. Dakota had been talking to Black and he was doing well. I had been so wrapped up in my little family that I had forgot about my other family, but we were slowly but surely going to get back right.

This situation with Chance was taking all of my energy. I knew he wasn't doing anything wrong being there with Adore, but I was just shocked at the time. What woman wouldn't have felt some type of way seeing her man with a woman that he had gotten pregnant? I knew in my heart that if anybody loved me and worshipped the ground that I walked on, it was Chance. It's crazy that it took my brother to make me realize it. Maybe we needed a new start and to get away from all this drama. I could only hope Dakota and his little family came along, seeing that he is so against leaving Atlanta. I know I told Chance that I needed space, but I didn't care about the negative things anymore, I was only focused on the positive and with him is where I wanted to be. We all we got.

Everybody around me was finally happy and that was enough for me to be happy about. I had yet to get the chance to catch up with Moe, and I needed to get all of the stress off of my chest. I just had to find a way to get in contact with her because it would be a cold day in hell before Chance would give me her number. The fact that I have an older sister kind of warmed my heart a little because that was something I always wanted, but it was so complicated now. True enough, it would take a hell of a lot to build a relationship with her since we had an altercation and I was now raising her son with the man I knew she still loved. Shit, we had more drama than a little bit. It was time for Chance to put all of this behind us and allow her to raise Christian because everybody makes mistakes and I hope she learned from them. I had so much hate in my heart for my mother and all of her secrets. Her and Roberto ruined our childhood, and whether they were dead or not, I would never forgive either of them. So much could have been prevented if we had parents that cared. I wouldn't be surprised if her ass wasn't dead, as much as she lied. I wanted to take my family out for dinner tonight, so I texted Chance to see if he wanted to go out.

Me: Be home in a few, want to go out.

Hubby: That's cool, what did you have in mind? You were pissed with a nigga a while ago.

Me: Had a change of heart. Let's go to Pappadeaux.

Hubby: Bet. Let me get the kids dressed so we will be ready. I love you ma, remember that. It's us...

Me: Never them...I love you too Chance McCray.

It was time to get my shit together. I had a wonderful man that loved me just as I was, so it was only right I did the same for him. Who didn't have flaws? Nobody is perfect, but Chance McCray was perfect enough for me. It was time I showed him just how much I loved and appreciated him. He was a great father to the kids and a great man for me. Fuck Adore and any other bitch that had him in the past, because Dior Baker is his present and his future. I was the reason our engagement was called off, but that was the old me. The new me was going to propose to my man and show him just how much he means to me. I got in my car and pulled off. I was turned up, riding down 75, headed home to my babies. I tried to stop at a red light and my brakes were going straight to the floor and failed to stop. I tried to swerve around another car and all of a sudden, everything went black.

Jas:

"Mmm, right there babe." Los was munching on his favorite dish and I was loving every minute of it. I had already cum three times, within five minutes.

"You like when I eat that pussy baby?" My words were caught in my throat, so I just nodded my head yes. I was so tempted to take the dick because I wanted it so badly. He had the prettiest mushroom head I had ever seen, and the way he stroked up and down with his hands made my mouth water.

"I'm about to cum bae, I can't take it." I tried scooting backwards, but he locked my legs into his arms so I couldn't move. He took a peppermint and sat it on his tongue, then inserted it into my opening. The tingling sensation sent me to an all new height.

"Ah, Los, what are you doing to me? Oh my God, geesh."

With the peppermint sitting at the tip of his tongue, he started flicking his tongue real fast on my clitoris, and I felt my body start shaking. I started squirting and he licked up every part of my juices. He stood up and went to the bathroom to clean himself off and I just laid there, temporarily paralyzed. I have never had that many orgasms in one day, let alone one hour. This man was dangerous for my body. I couldn't wait to have this baby and my six weeks to run up because I needed what his boxers were holding. He came and laid beside me and laid my head on his chest. I started tracing my finger down his sexy, toned chest.

"Babe, thank you for riding this pregnancy out with me. I know you get tired of eating this kitty and not being able to stroke it with nothing but that tongue." He looked at me and started laughing.

"Girl bye, you sound crazy as fuck. I aim to please and I know you want this dick just as bad. A nigga told you he was fucking with you and I meant it. You good ma, but on the real, that pussy should come with a caution sign though. I know she lethal. That thang be gripping a nigga tongue, keeping it all warm and shit." I couldn't help but blush.

"Well, I don't mean to toot my own horn, but she is the best. I know how to put shit down, but you're going to find out just how lethal she is."

"Is that right? On some real shit though ma, a nigga really feeling you. I haven't been in a relationship since my baby mama, but I could see what we got going on going somewhere. I'm used to dogging hoes and sending them on their way, but I've been caked up with your ass for about four months now and a nigga really loving that shit.

"Let me find out you catching feelings for lil Jas with the fat ass." I looked up at him and he kissed me on the forehead. I was falling hard for this man and I could no longer control it. The way he treated me spoke volumes.

"Can I ask you a question?"

"Anytime."

"The last time I asked, you brushed it off. What happened to you and your baby mama?"

"She started doing drugs and stole from me so that she could get high. She's been clean since she had my son, but I'm not fucking with her. Any bitch that could turn to drugs and steal from you to support her habit is not a bitch I want to be with."

"That's deep babe."

"So tell me about you and your daughter's father."

I always avoided this conversation because I didn't want him or anyone else to judge me. I knew I had to tell him about it one day, I just didn't expect it to be so soon.

"I have known Dakota and Dior since we were in middle school. They always had my back and treated me like a sister, since my family was so fucked up. After high school, I moved to Baltimore for college and we kind of drifted apart. Dakota started back calling and came to visit me a few times and we started messing around. Dior never knew about it until I got pregnant. I found out about Bree and he basically just ended things with us."

"Damn, that's fucked up babe. You know Daddy Los got you."

Crazy thing about it was, I knew he had me, I just never wanted him to let me go.

Chapter 20

Chance:

Beckford had just called and given a nigga some good news about Cali. The prosecutor had a change of heart and requested that she did six months with two months time served, so she would be home in four. Everybody was about money, so it was nothing to throw him a million to show favor to her. I still had not talked to my sister or my mother, but I was headed their way. I didn't understand what the fuck Chas' problem was and why she was giving Cali the cold shoulder, that wasn't like her at all. Both of the kids were sleeping, so I got them out of the car and took them in the house and laid them down. I walked into the kitchen and she was on the phone with somebody, talking shit like always. I couldn't believe what the fuck I overheard her saying.

"Honey, I'm going to let her sit her little stupid ass in there. She wants to be grown, chasing that no good ass nigga around, then let his ass help her out. She calls here every damn day, but I have nothing to say to her. She ain't no good, just like her no good ass daddy. You know he married to some white woman now, right? If Cali knew who his bitch ass was, I would send her ass to live with him."

I was furious as fuck listening to my mama dog my sister out and confess that we didn't share the same father. I picked up the vase and threw it past her head and the glass shattered on impact. She screamed because it scared her, then she turned towards me.

"HANG UP THE FUCKING PHONE RIGHT NOW!" I felt the tears rolling down my face. I felt my blood boiling.

"Chance, I can explain."

"FUCK THAT. SO POPS WASN'T CALI'S DAD?" She looked down towards the floor and shook her head no. If this wasn't my mother, I would choke her ass with my bare hands. She betrayed this whole family. I knew there was a reason Cali didn't have the same last name as me and Chas, and she was the only one that had different color eyes.

"Son, I'm sorry you had to find out this way. I cheated on your father and got pregnant. When I told her father I was pregnant, he told me to get rid of her because he was in love with some white woman. I couldn't do it, so I just went through with it and told your father she was his. I swear I never meant to hurt you."

"Nah, you mean you never meant for me to find out. This that bullshit. I learn something new with your ass every week. That is your daughter ma, how could you leave her out there to fend for herself? She never did shit to you for her to be treated like that, and where the fuck is Chas?"

"Chas isn't here, but please listen to me." I wasn't up for a story full of lies from my mother, I couldn't trust her. My phone started ringing and it was Jas calling. I didn't know what the fuck she could be calling for this late at night.

"YEAH!"

"Chance, get to the hospital quick. It's Dior, there's been an accident."

I couldn't breathe. The room was spinning.

"Chance, did you hear me damn it?"

"What hospital?"

"Emory." I hung up without even responding. I had to get to my baby. I left the kids with my mom, even though I was pissed with her, but that shit was minor right about now. I had to get to Dior, she needed me. I did the whole dash all the way there, running through stop lights and everything. I pulled up to the hospital and jumped out, leaving my car sitting in the front, not giving a fuck if it got towed. When I ran in, I saw Dakota, Bree, and Jasmine sitting there.

"What the fuck happened? Where is my baby?"

"Calm down man. I know this shit got your mind all types of fucked up. She hit a power pole somehow. We're just waiting on word from the doctor." I sat down with my head in my hands and I was shaking. I was losing it. Here I was, waiting on my baby to get home and she never made it. Dior was my world and I would die if something happened to her. We sat in the waiting room for an hour and I was getting frustrated. I jumped up and walked over to the nurses' station.

"Yo, what the fuck taking so long for the doctor to come out? I need you to get your ass back there and see what the fuck going on with my wife."

"Sir, I need for you to calm down. The doctor should be out shortly." I started pacing back and forth and I felt myself breaking down. It was killing me that I didn't know what was going on. Every time you turn around, we at a fucking hospital. I was over all this shit.

"Are you the family of Dior Baker?"

We all stepped up to see what the doctor had to say. I just know whatever he had to say better had been good news.

"As you know, she was in a terrible accident, which caused her left leg to be broken and her jaw bone. She had slight internal bleeding, but we managed to stop it. Surprisingly, the fetus survived all of the trauma."

Dakota stepped around me, "Fetus? MY sister pregnant, again?"

"Yes, sir. It survived, but she needs a lot of rest, her body is weak and tired. You can go see her, two at a time, but I must warn you, she is highly sedated."

I ran to the back, not even worried about who was coming with me. When I walked into the room and saw my baby hooked up to all this bullshit, I started boohoo crying like a little bitch. I didn't even give a fuck though. It felt like the walls were closing in on me. Jasmine came in and ran over to Dior, crying. This was all fucked up. How did my baby hit a pole? My life was falling harder and harder and it was killing me. We sat for a couple of hours before two detectives came in. They informed us that the accident wasn't actually an accident and that her brake line was somehow cut. They asked did we have any idea who would do this, but I ain't no snitch bitch and

I would handle shit on my own. They ended up leaving when they saw a nigga wasn't telling they ass shit. As far as they know, I didn't know shit. I sat down, thinking about who could do something like this and try to take Dior from me. My brother was dead and he was the only person I could think of. I don't have beef with nobody and the fact that my baby was at the hospital majority of that day, only left one person in mind.

"I'm going to kill that bitch!"

Jasmine jumped when I started yelling and pacing back and forth. "Kill who?"

I didn't even answer her. I ran out the door and it was about to be a major thot blood bath. I ran out of the hospital and hopped in my truck and peeled off. This bitch was about to feel it. Nobody fucks with my girl and gets away with it. I pulled up to the hotel ten minutes later and hopped out. I started beating on her door, not giving a fuck who else was here. She opened the door and smiled like shit was all good and I punched that bitch dead in her mouth, causing her to fall backwards.

"Let's go, NOW."

She held her hands up in the surrender stand and we walked out. I was not a fool to do anything with cameras and shit around. I led her to my car, and we got in and took off. I pulled up to one of my warehouses and told her to get out. I made a phone call to my cleanup crew and told them to pull up in five.

"Why you do it, huh?" She started crying, but that shit meant absolutely nothing to me.

"Why couldn't you just love me? What did she have that I didn't?" I looked at her with tears in my eyes because all I could see was Dior laid up in that hospital bed.

"Me." I gave her two personal bullets to the head. I waited for the crew to pull up, got in my truck and left, just as fast as I came. I spared nobody when it came to my family, and what Adore never understood was, she could never have me.

Cody:

A nigga's heart was hurting, seeing my sister like this. I knew it was more to the story than what I was told, but I would find out soon enough. Jasmine had called and told me about the detectives saying the accident was a murder attempt, and it really fucked me up. I had been here with my sister all day. She woke up a little, but she was still in a lot of pain. I sent Bree home to get the boys from the nanny and I was headed out to get more information. When I was walking out, I saw Roberto walking in with some older lady and a creepy looking ass man. They started walking towards me. "What the fuck are you doing here? Who called you?"

The lady stepped in front of my dad, "Dakota, this is not the time for this. We just came to see Dior." I didn't even know who she was, so she had no reason to even be talking to me.

"Don't tell me what it is not the time for. Shit, who are you anyway?"

"Dakota, I am your grandmother Pauline." When I was younger, I heard stories about her, but I had never met her, so in my eyes, she wasn't no kin to me. I wasn't interested in getting to know her. All I was worried about was who did this to my sister.

"We never met you, so why you coming up in here like you care about my sister? She doesn't give a damn about seeing none of y'all motherfuckers."

My dad walked in my personal space, "I know you have your little issues with me, but you will not talk to my mother that way. You will respect her and talk like you have some damn sense." I laughed at this nigga. I know damn well he didn't come up in here like he was a real father and try to make demands. I wasn't moved at all.

"You not shit to me or my sister. Y'all can exit stage left, the same way you came in, because seeing her is not going to happen. I don't trust your ass and I don't even know her, so she ain't seeing her either. Only way y'all will see her is if I go back there with you."

"That will be fine. I just want to make sure she is okay." I stood there staring at them, until I finally decided to take them back there. They only had five minutes, whether they knew it or not. We walked into my sister's room and she was sleep, until she heard us come in. She looked from me to my dad, to my alleged grandmother. Her eyes shot wide open when she looked at the man that came with them, and she started panicking. She snatched the IV out of her arm. I ran to the side of the bed.

"Dior, calm down, what's wrong?" She attempted to point her finger, but failed because of the pain. Three of the nurses ran in and told us to leave. The guy with my pops was smiling and it pissed me off.

"Yo my man, what the fuck is so funny? Why the fuck did my sister just panic when she saw you?" Something was not right and I was mad as fuck because I didn't know what was going on. I hate my sister was still high off those meds and couldn't tell me shit.

"Son, calm down, I don't know why she acted that way. She probably thought she'd seen him before, that's all."

"Get the fuck out, and don't come back. We were just fine until you brought your trifling ass back around. Stay the fuck away from us nigga." I was furious. I went to the nurses' desk and told them nobody was allowed back there but me, Chance, Jas, and Bree. I was going to find out why the fuck my sister was so scared of that nigga. I was leaving the hospital when I saw them bringing a pregnant woman in, and she was in labor. It didn't dawn on me until they were up close that the woman was Jas. My anger soon faded away, my baby girl was on her way.

Jas:

When I tell y'all this labor shit ain't no joke, I mean it. I didn't see how bitches did this shit like it was a hobby. I was at home, getting the best head of my life, when my water broke. Disgusting, right? I wasn't due for five more weeks, but I guess my baby girl decided otherwise. We both panicked and he brought me to the hospital. I told him he could leave because I knew that Dakota was here and I didn't want any drama. That was why I appreciated my baby so much because he didn't trip and was willing to be in there with me through it all. If you ain't never had a real nigga, you better get you one. The nurses rushed me in on a stretcher and I locked eyes with Dakota and he ran to my side. I really appreciated him for keeping his word and being there, regardless of our situation. I wish Dior was in the position to be in the room with me like we had planned. I knew she would be so hurt that she missed this moment. Dakota was holding my hand and rubbing his fingers through my scalp, and I have to admit it soothed me.

"Everything is going to be alright Jas. You are strong and you can handle this. Small thing to a giant, you got it ma." I was in so much pain to tell him, but I really appreciated his words of encouragement. All I could do was nod my head. I felt sweat dripping down my face and he wet a towel with cold water and dabbed my face with it. My contractions were coming back to back and I couldn't take it anymore. I had planned to do a natural birth, but I went ahead and told them I wanted the epidural. It helped the pain a little bit, but I was still feeling the contractions every time they came. I knew at that moment I would never get pregnant again. The doctor came in and told me I was now eight centimeters and to get myself prepared to push when I got to ten. I was sweating bullets because I was so nervous. My mind started wandering off to the last time I talked with my mother.

Thirteen years old:

"Jazzy, come sit down so I can talk to you about the birds and the bees."

"Birds and bees? Mommy, I don't want to talk about animals."

"No, no silly. That is just what the old folks used to call it. You see, when you get a boyfriend at age sixteen, not a day sooner, I don't want you to be in the dark about sex."

"I take sex education classes at school mommy."

"I know baby, but these little boys will trick you into having sex and get you pregnant, then leave you. If you're going to have sex, always use protection and still be cautious."

That was the last thing I remember talking about. I never talked about my mommy because it was such a touchy subject. She passed away a week after that conversation from stomach cancer. I never even knew she was sick.

"Jas, you hear the doctor?"

Dakota snapped me out of my thoughts. It was time for me to push. After only five pushes, I delivered a healthy 5lbs. 6oz., chocolate baby girl. I instantly fell in love with Demi Nichole Baker.

Chapter 21

Rue:

I've been on the back side for a minute, but it's time for me to speak the fuck up. I am Nyrue, better known as Rue, the biggest coke and marijuana distributor in Miami. My father was the biggest drug lord and leader of a French cartel over in Paris, so I came from money. He didn't want me to go this route with my life, but when I saw how he was eating, I had to get in. I own a studio in Atlanta and am in the process of getting another one built. I moved down here to the city on business, but when I met Cali, it turned into pleasure. When I met Cali five years ago, I knew she was the one for me. She was so beautiful and those green eyes caught ahold of my heart from the beginning. She was slim, but that ass was something I couldn't get my mind off of. I knew when I first met her that I wanted her to be my wife. We had our hard times of course, when a nigga was fucking different bitches, thinking it was something out there better. After she left me that last time, I learned not to take her for granted. She even thought I didn't know about the two abortions that she had gotten. We both did some fucked up shit to each other, but killing my seeds and not telling me about it was fucked up. I've been faithful these past three and a half years. Her sister Chasity ain't nothing but a little hoe, and I don't like her ass. I felt like shit because I've been keeping a secret from Cali for two years and I'm tired of hiding this shit. Chasity be kicking it like she doesn't like a nigga whenever Cali is around, but be pulling up at my crib, trying to throw that little pussy at me. I can't lie, I almost slipped up and fucked one night when we all went out and got drunk. They had gone home, but Chasity came back and seduced me. She sucked my dick and tried to sit on my rod, but I pushed her ass off me. She went on and on about how she was better than Cali and Cali didn't deserve me, but I wasn't no fool. I didn't know what would make her ass think I could take her serious when she could betray her sister and try to fuck her nigga. Cali would beat the shit out of both of us if she knew. My baby was a rider, any day and time, and I fucked with her strong for that. When I first met her, I wasn't nearly as successful as I am now, but she overlooked it and accepted me for me. When she took that charge for me, I was pissed off, but I knew she wouldn't have that shit any other way. I've been running this check up, so when she came home, we would be straight. I know she's pissed with a nigga because she hasn't heard from me, but a nigga trying to have me and my wife living lovely. As for her punk ass brother, he didn't even know his connect was my father, and he fucked with the wrong nigga. I was about to put a stop to his money flow.

Cali:

I had done so much thinking about my life and everybody around me that it wasn't even funny. I was still fucked up about my sister and Rue's situation, and I didn't know who I could trust. I just shut everybody out and stopped calling home because I got tired of the unanswered calls. I appreciated my brother more than ever after Beckford told me I had four months to go. Everybody that shitted on me while I was in here, would soon feel the wrath of Cali. I was heartbroken that I took this charge for Rue and he basically turned his back on me. Any other bitch would have snitched on a nigga, but not me, I rode it out. When it came to Chasity, I had a whole different agenda for her trifling ass. When I finally got out of here, it was going to be a brand new me and I doubt anybody was going to like it. I couldn't wait to meet my niece Cayleigh and spoil her rotten. That was the only good thing I had planned once my release date came.

It was finally time for me to be released from jail and I was ecstatic. So many lessons were learned and I found out who would ride for me. I didn't call Chance to come get me because I had some business to take care of. I rode the bus over to Nyrue's studio, since it wasn't far from the jail. I spotted his car and dinged the bell for the bus to stop. I walked in the studio and the smell of gas hit me instantly. I walked to the back and there my no good, so-called boyfriend was. He didn't even see me walk in.

"So that's how you do? Get a bitch to take a charge for you, then turn your back on her?"

He turned around like a deer caught in headlights.

"Calz, what's up bae, when you come home?" He reached for me and I pushed him back.

"Don't fucking touch me with your fake ass. If you would have ridden it out with me, you would have known when I was getting out. But nah, you had to be the same Nyrue that I met and put the streets before me. I came here to let you that was real foul Rue and I don't want shit else to do with you. You're not the real nigga I thought you were because a real nigga would have stuck by his lady's side. I got out with intentions to swing on your ass, but you're not even worth it my nigga." I turned to walk away, then turned back around, "Oh yeah, and I know about you and my sister. You kept that shit away from me, thinking you would get away with it, but nah nigga, you caught."

"Cali, baby, you know a nigga—" I cut his ass off, because right now, his words didn't mean shit to me. I left out on a mission, Chasity was about to get these hands.

Los:

I know y'all ain't think we were going to end this shit without the boss introducing himself. I'm Carlos, and nah I'm not a drug dealer like the rest of these fuck niggas. I'm too got damn old for that shit. I'm 32 years old and I own five construction companies. I have two in Atlanta, one in Florida, one in Tennessee, and one in New Orleans. I've been out of the game for a few years now. I was a real hot head, nothing like these niggas portray to be. I was on some kill the whole family type of shit when it came to this bread. When I got locked up and had to serve five years, but was facing twenty-five to life, I knew I had to get out. I caught eleven bodies while I was hustling and while the shit felt good doing it, I still felt like shit afterwards. I got two kids with a bomb bitch that ain't got shit going on with her life. Jasmine, on the other hand, is like a breath of fresh air. Shawty was a real bitch and I rocked with her the long way. I have never fucked with a bitch as hard as I fuck with her, and I wasn't even getting the pussy. I fucked a few broads from time to time because I wasn't on no celibate shit. If she ever found out, I expected her to understand. I thought her baby daddy was going to bring a nigga out of retirement and get himself in a body bag with that mouth he got. When I first met her, I was on some revenge type of shit because I knew them niggas she rolls with killed my cousin. Yeah, that's right, I'm Marco's first cousin. I came to the city after I saw my cousin on the news and they said he was murdered in cold blood. That was my intentions, but a nigga can't even lie, I slipped and fell in love with Jas. Now I'm on some fuck all the drama type shit, I just want to be happy with my girl. I told that nigga from the start to let that shit go with his brother anyways because it wasn't his fault, but Marco was a hardheaded ass nigga. I can't lie though, I did fuck Chance's little sister from time to time. She's a thot and I wouldn't wife her or no shit like that. Chasity was sneaky and I could tell. I would just fuck her, throw her a few stacks, and put her ass out. I really cut her ass off when she started telling me all kinds of bullshit about how she was in love with her sister's nigga and she put a bug in the police's ear about her sister transporting drugs. She said her sister was doing time for that shit and that's when I knew she wasn't a bitch I needed around me, even though I was legit. Jas was supposed to be released from the hospital later on, so I was chilling until my baby called. I didn't know how this shit was going to work having to be around her smart mouth ass baby daddy. He talked shit just like a female, and niggas with bitch tendencies I steer clear from. I'm about getting money, but I had an objective for Chance. Either he would get down or lay down.

Stay Tuned…

Part 3 coming soon

Made in the USA
Middletown, DE
07 October 2022

12242988R00085